Clark Henry Bronson

The sparkling light and other poems

Clark Henry Bronson

The sparkling light and other poems

ISBN/EAN: 9783337269265

Printed in Europe, USA, Canada, Australia, Japan

Cover: Foto ©Andreas Hilbeck / pixelio.de

More available books at **www.hansebooks.com**

THE SPARKLING LIGHT

AND OTHER POEMS

BY

C. H. BRONSON.

WITH ILLUSTRATIONS.

MANCHESTER, IOWA:
PUBLISHED BY THE AUTHOR.
1877.

TO MY WIFE

THIS, MY FIRST LITERARY EFFORT,

IS RESPECTFULLY DEDICATED.

PREFACE.

DURING the author's career as a lecturer, he sometimes repeated one or two poems, of his own composition, in the presence of his audiences; these were so highly appreciated, and the author received so many flattering encomiums, that he became vain enough to suppose that, perhaps, they might contain some merit, and besides he was so beset with applications for copies, which from lack of time he was unable to furnish, that he resolved to write and publish a number of poems for the benefit of his audiences, and this book is the result. None of these poems have ever before been written or published, and but one of them — The Sparkling Light — has been repeated to audiences. Some of the poems, which refer to scientific topics, are different from any that as yet have come within the author's observation. That this work contains many errors and imperfections the author is well aware, and as to whether they are overbalanced by its excellencies or not, the public will be the best judge. But in either case, the author has done the best that he could according to his natural capacity and the limited amount of time taken in its composition.

C. H. BRONSON.

A BRIEF ACCOUNT OF THE AUTHOR.

IN order to gratify a natural curiosity which, under the circumstances, many people seem pleased to manifest, the following brief account of the author is deemed advisable : He was born on the 11th of October, 1845, at Lee Centre, a small town near the city of Rome, Oneida county, New York. In 1855 his parents removed to Iowa City, Iowa, which at that time was the capital of the State. At the age of eighteen the author, while attending the university at the latter place, had the misfortune to suddenly and unexpectedly lose his sight; this great calamity, this total loss of vision, was caused by excessive study at night, and subsequent improper treatment by physicians. Previous to this affliction the author had paid considerable attention to phrenology, as well as geology, zoology, and other branches of natural history. Immediately after meeting with his misfortune he commenced energetically to prepare himself for a lecturer upon these important subjects. He entered the field at the age of twenty-one, and has been engaged in this important work ever since. In his profession of phrenologist and lecturer his success has been more than equal to his expectations, and he has been highly appreciated by the public wherever he has prosecuted his work. His field has been principally confined to the States of Iowa, Illinois, Wisconsin, Minnesota, Missouri, Nebraska, Kansas and Texas, in many parts of all these he is well known.

CONTENTS.

11

THE SPARKLING LIGHT.

THE SPARKLING LIGHT.

HAVE you seen the Light, the glorious Light,
    As it flies from the sun dispelling the night?
From its pathway fades all darkness and gloom,
It lights up the palace, it blesses the tomb;
The meanest beggar that travels the street
It gently enfolds in its diamond sheet.
The rich and the poor, the young and the old,
Alike are entwined in its shining fold.
The world lost convict in his dreary cell
Would be entombed in a living hell,
Would pine and die, in the endless night,
Were it not for the Light, the glorious Light,
That bursts in through the prison grate
And thus enlivens his dreary fate.

Have you seen the Light, the glorious Light?
How it startles the fancy with visions bright,
Awakening hopes of future bliss,
As the dew-dropped flowers it stoops to kiss
In the early morn, when it kills the night,
The beautiful, blessed, Sparkling Light?

15

Have you seen the Light, the glorious Light?
When the earth puts on her mantle of white,
As it gilds the iced crystals on the trees,
And the snowflakes fluttering in the breeze,
And the old church steeple that towers so high
That its spire is a glittering bead in the sky,
And the distant mountains that loom so grand
That they seem in the distance a fairy land?
Naught could the caged bird's grief assuage
If from the light you take its cage;
If from its eyes you pluck the sight
Its greatest boon would be for Light;
That carols o'er earth in its joyous flight,
Awakening scenes of days gone by,
As it floods the soul from the sun and sky
In the gentle eve when it hails the night,
The beautiful, blessed, Sparkling Light.

I once saw the Light, the glorious Light,
And the beauties of nature all beamed on my sight,
But *grim darkness* came in her terrible gloom
And bound me for life, in a living tomb;
I struggled and fought, but 'twas all in vain,
To drive her away from my aching brain;
The contest was brief, though I struggled and fought
With a soul on fire, it was all for naught;

And when all was over, grim darkness was there,
And she waved o'er my head her black wings of despair,
And she bound me down with her robes of night
And closed forever my gates of Light.
The beautiful world faded out of my sight,
And the sun rose up, and the sun sank down,
And the stars came out, and the moon looked on,
But my world stood still in its endless night,
For lost was the beautiful, Sparkling Light.

2

THE ASHTABULA DISASTER.

IT was on the twenty-ninth day of December,
  In the great Centennial year,
An accident happened, that many remember,
  And there still flows the silent tear
For those, who on that dread day were hurled
Out of this, into a better world;
And mourning badges are still unfurled.

'Twas past seven o'clock, the night was advancing
  And casting her shadows around,
When lo! from the East a great red eye came glancing,
  The head-light of the train West bound:
And now the long train comes into view,
She moves along so steady and true
With two great engines to pull her through.

What a glorious sight is the swift-rushing train,
    smoothly she glides o'er the rail;
From her head, there burst clouds of steam, smoke, and flame,
  That trails far behind like a vail.

A sound of thunder with rapid peals,
A clank of iron, a whirr of wheels,
The great earth trembles the shock she feels.

There are women and men on that ill-fated train,
    The high and lowly, the young and old,
There are maids that are pretty, and maids that are plain,
    Some are timid and others bold.
And there is one, with long waving hair,
With diamond eyes and a form so fair,
A model of beauty, rich and rare.

She is bound for the West, where her lover, her choice,
    Is awaiting a New Year's bride.
The trousseau is ready, how two fond hearts rejoice,
    And hope soon to beat side by side;
But alas! on earth, they ne'er will meet,
She rushes along grim death to greet,
Her wedding trousseau a winding-sheet.

And one is a Doctor, whose patients are waiting
    His wonderful medical skill;
His wife and his children in fancy creating
    The picture his presence would fill:
But patients will wait, and wait in vain,
Both wife and children will feel a pain
That during life will ever remain.

And one is a Lawyer of great technical skill,
 With a shrewd, cunning eye of gray;
What is stored in his mind a great volume would fill,
 But he'll take his long rest to-day.
No more, to appear at earthly bars,
No more, to trouble with human jars,
No more, to shine among legal stars.

And one is a Preacher, whose thoughts are of Heaven,
 And saving the sinners of earth,
Who joyously thinks of the souls he will leaven
 And quicken, to meet the new birth;
No more to mortals of earth he'll preach,
No more exhort, and no more beseech,
For soon the pearly gates he will reach.

And one is a Merchant, always ready to sell
 At the lowest prices for cash;
He has had a large trade, he feels happy and well,
 With never a fear of a smash;
But no more profit or loss he'll trace,
A stranger will take his usual place,
And buyers will miss his genial face.

And one is a Farmer, who has just been down East
 To visit the old folks at home,
And now back to his farm, for he fears that some beast
 May chance in his absence to roam;

But cattle and hogs, no more he'll keep,
No more he'll sow, and no more he'll reap,
For soon he will take his long, last sleep.

There are fathers and mothers on the train to-night,
    With babes and little children dear,
How their hearts beat with hope, they are filled with delight,
    As they think of the coming New Year;
Both father and child will soon go down,
Both mother and babe will wear a crown,
And there will be weeping, through the town.

Now in front of the train, there's a bridge long and high,
    For a terrible chasm it leaps,
To the view, a great cobweb is dotting the sky
    As swift o'er the vision it creeps.
It looks too fragile to stand the strain,
The immense weight of that heavy train,
But for years across the gulf it has lain.

And o'er it in safety many thousands of trains
    Quickly passed to the other side,
And the hundreds on board have no thought in their brains,
    That this is a terrible ride.
And now the long train its freight has bore
On to the bridge, just one minute more
And all will have passed in safety o'er.

But a minute of time, is enough for grim death
    To send from his nostrils a flame
That will burn out the life, that will stifle the breath,
    And leave naught behind but the name.
The great bridge totters beneath the weight,
Oh! God! it falls with its precious freight,
And all go down to a dreadful fate.

Oh! what sickening sounds resound through the air,
    As down into that dark abyss
Plunged cars, timbers and rails, as swift downward they tear,
    With the engine's horrible hiss,
Turning and whirling, downward they dash,
Striking the ground with a deafening crash,
All mixing in one great monstrous smash.

Cries, groans and shrieks, burst forth a chilling, rending flood
    From the writhing and twisting heap,
And from its base, there spurt small streams of human blood,
    Staining the ground with crimson deep,
Flowing from this great funeral bed,
By human beings its sources fed,
Flowing from wounded, dying and dead.

Like the ants from their hills, crawl the uninjured few,
    Unchained, from this vast hill of death,
They're so dazed by the shock, that they nothing can do;
    And before they've regained their breath,

From many places in that great heap
Fiery tongues of flame were seen to leap,
'Twas enough to make the angels weep.

Imprisoned, entombed, in that dread funeral pyre
    There are many, who still would live
If they could be released from their bondage of fire,
    But poor mortals no aid can give.
And now the fierce flames are rising higher,
As hotter grows the funeral pyre,
With wails and moans the victims expire.

In that narrow, deep, gulch it was dreadful to die,
    All cut off from the outside world
By its vertical walls, with a small strip of sky
    O'er its mouth a mantle unfurled.
The surging flames, the sickening smell,
The awful sounds from that crater well,
All formed a perfect picture of hell.

Many came, who lived near the scene of disaster
    And climbed down the vertical stair,
And with the survivors attempted to master
    That terrible hell of despair;
Although they worked with all of their might
The flames were the victors of the fight,
For many were burned alive that night.

Some of those that survived, as they stood near the wreck
    Without the least power to save,
Saw a harrowing sight, that all pleasures will check
    And will haunt them into the grave,
Fathers and mothers saw children dear
Burning alive, and yet were so near
That their agonized shrieks they could hear.

There were wives, that had husbands, and husbands had
    wives,
    Who forever were cut in twain
By those death-dealing flames, that like poisonous knives
    Inflicted incurable pain.
Some had to be held in their despair,
Some fainted away, some tore their hair,
And many showed insanities glare.

At length, the grim fire fiend has no more to devour
    And quietly sinks to his rest;
Yet, he hisses and smokes as he yields to the power
    By which his cursed life is suppressed.
He leaves behind but a blackened heap,
A hideous grave where many sleep,
And heart-broke mourners their vigils keep.

What a long, long night, but the morning is breaking
    And now a sad task must be done;

With their shovels and hoes the workers are raking,
  Exhuming the dead has begun,
A hand, an arm, a foot, or a head,
Pieces and fragments, parts of the dead,
And sometimes only a single shred.

Many bodies were found so consumed by the flames
  That not even a single trace
That would tell who they were, where they lived, or their
      names,
  With twenty-seven this was the case;
And there were some cremated entire,
Resolved to dust in that raging fire,
And who they were, may never transpire.

Of one cremated man, there was found but a key,
  Recognized by many a friend,
Had it not been for this, what a dark mystery
  Would his disappearance attend,
None living saw him go on that train,
And friends his absence could not explain
Till the key was found, then all was plain.

Of another was found but a small pocket knife
  To tell his sad story of death;
For his physical form disappeared with his life
  As if it had been but a breath;

But the knife was left to tell the tale
Of horror, that makes the cheek turn pale,
And causes many to weep and wail.

At the end of three days when this sad work was o'er,
    Then the coroner's jury came
And viewed all that was left, of full many a score
    That went down to death on the train;
They rendered their verdict, very plain,
" The bridge was too weak to stand the strain
And hence, it went down with all the train;

" That the stoves on the cars were not properly made
    To quench all their fire when o'erturned;'
That to this cause the great conflagration is laid,
    By which means so many were burned;
That the Railroad Co. showed great neglect,
Neither life nor laws did they respect
And all the damage on them reflect."

Thus ends this awful tale of misery and death,
    And the half has never been told
Of this horrible theme, which yields in its every breath
    Sighs of the grave, so dark and cold.
And as years glide along in their flight,
What occurred on that terrible night
Never will fade from memory's sight.

GOING IT BLIND.

As I drift along "o'er life's troubled sea"
    This rhythmical song is whispered to me,—
It floats in the air, above and below,
Now here and now there, wherever I go;
'Tis sung with a wail, 'tis sung with delight,
By the moonbeams pale, and the sun's bright light,
By those who revel, by those who rail
And glide o'er the level with wide-spread sail.
The reckless and bold as they hurry along,
With the young and old all join in the song,
And this is the strain, as I call it to mind,
With might and with main, we are Going it Blind.

Ah! many there are, who are Going it Blind,
You need not go far examples to find;
Just look at that man of majestic parts,
Dame Nature outran, are subtlest arts.
His body in moulding, his brain and his mind,
His genius unfolding, his nature refine,
Advantages bright have followed his birth,
A bright, shining light might he be on the earth.

"BUT HE TAKES TO STRONG DRINK, AND DOWN HE DOES GO,
OH HEAVENS! TO THINK HE HAS FALLEN SO LOW."

But he takes to strong drink, and down he does go,
Oh Heavens! to think he has fallen so low;
But the fact is plain, his star has declined,
For with might and with main, he is Going it Blind.

Behold! that fair maid, on whose cheek the rose tint
Of beauty is laid by Nature's imprint,
With soft eyes that charm by their lustrous light,
With hand, neck and arm of snowiest white;
From her shapely feet to her crested head.
A vision complete with perfections spread.
Ah! 'tis sad to find that a form so fair
Oft contains a mind that cannot compare

With the home where it dwells, in beauty and worth;
What a sad tale it tells of wrong training from birth,
Where prudence is wanting, affection is blind,
And vice with its vaunting soon follows behind;
Our judgment and reason may be e'er so bright,
But not used in season they withhold their light:
It is after you fall, when dark is your sun,
That they often recall what might have been done.
Thus with this fair maid, when the tempter has come,
His game has been played and his victory won;
She has tripped and fell, she has blasted her name,
And she drinks at the well of remorse and shame;
Oh! black is the stain of virtue resigned,
For with might and with main, she is Going it Blind.

Some husbands and wives are Going it Blind,
Their domestic lives are of such a kind
That happiness dies as they drift apart,
And affection's ties, one by one, depart;
The husband, his wife, in trying to rule
By discord and strife, is only a fool.
To manage a wife is simple and plain
But many through life find their efforts vain:
First know yourself well, your temper to keep,
You'll master one hell and put it to sleep.
To master your wife just study her heart,
Her nature, her life, in every part;

Then o'er her faults throw the mantle of love,
The change may be slow, but she will improve,
And soon learn to go as you touch the bit,
But go very slow, or the rule wont fit.
If husbands and wives would all the time try
To lead peaceful lives, of sweet harmony,
The banner of love would soon be unfurled
And soaring aloft, would conquer the world.
But women and men will quarrel and fight,
Again and again, from morning till night,
'Tis an awful strain on the human mind
For with might and main they are Going it Blind.

The Capitalists are Going it Blind,
The Laboring grists, in trying to grind
To so fine a pitch, that the working man
Is down in the ditch, with his pick and pan
From morning till night, in all kinds of weather,
With all of his might, to keep together
His body and soul, and that of his brood;
And this on the whole is by far too good,
So Capital thinks, for hewers of wood
Whose meats and whose drinks he would squelch if he could,
Compel them to live on nothing but air,
For labor must give with nothing to spare.
To educate man to work without pay
Is Capital's plan, and this is the way,

He orders the Firm to put on the screw
For only a term, to see if it will do,
Though Labor may groan, if she stands the strain,
Down near to the bone, she is pressed again,
At first, there is docked only ten per cent.,
Though Labor is shocked, she gives her consent,
And pinches to save, the loss to bridge o'er,
But another shave takes ten per cent. more.
Thus round and around, still turns the great screw,
And Labor the ground with her tears bedew.
In Capital's eyes, man is but a machine,
That without supplies will work slick and clean;
Without coal or oil its great maw to fill,
Would the engine toil at Capital's will?
No: 'twould lay and rust ere a wheel be driven,
For a *something* must for *something* be given,
But Capital knows of no such rule
And blusters, and blows like a pigheaded fool,
And will not refrain from starving mankind
For with might and main, He is Going it Blind.

And Labor, of course, is Going it Blind,
By using brute force its chains to unbind,
For the brain and mind are the powers that reign,
And muscle we find exerted in vain.
All the strikes and mobs to stop the evil
Are just like corn cobs thrown at the devil;

For they serve to make the matter still worse,
And Labor must take her place in the hearse.
For if there is a scare, Cap. shuts up his shop,
And all the work there, comes to a dead stop.
The factories shut down, the railroads won't build,
Both country and town with the tramps are filled,
For Cap. will not throw his money away,
He goes very slow, when the devil's to pay,
To fight against mind, our mind we must use,
But many we find who their powers abuse.
This land of free schools can have no excuse
For thousands of fools, who are its produce;
Not fools by their birth or lowly station,
But fools from a dearth of Education.
This ignorant class, with its brains asleep
Like a stupid ass, or a flock of sheep,
Is led here and there by more active brains.
Who take up the fare and handle the reins,
Who grind out the thought and dole out the grist,
And thus, they are taught just how to exist.
If Labor would send her children to school,
And never unbend from this urgent rule;
Develop their brains with powers of thought,
By taking some pains, with what they are taught.
If Labor would learn to use her own brain,
Her liberty earn, 'twould not be in vain;

3

Intelligence, skills the Laborer's hand,
Intelligence, fills with light the whole land.
But Labor will drink, and quarrel, and fight,
Neglecting to think or steer herself right,
She'll vote for the man, who talks very slick;
If this is her plan, in the ditch she will stick.
It seems very plain, she is far behind,
For with might and main, she is Going it Blind.

YES: I LOVE TOBACCO.

YES: I love Tobacco,
    And yet, full well I know
It injures me.
When I was but a boy
Sly smokes, I did enjoy,
With none to see.

The first trial made me sick,
Though 'twas hard I did stick,
'Twas stolen fruit.
Other boys had been sick,
Tried again, took the trick,
I followed suit.

I was thrashed, made to howl,
Had to face many a scowl,
But brassed it through;
The more closely I was held
So much more I rebelled,
And so would you.

Liberty, I did claim
And obtained just the same,
I would be free;
I would not be a slave,
Nor be taught to behave,
'Twas bad for me.

Soon I was habit's slave,
Liberty could not save,
The weed was king;
I was bound, golden chains,
Many joys, many pains,
I was a thing.

When to manhood I had grown,
All wild oats I had sown,
Habit still reigned:
Thrice in life I broke the chain
But it lured me back again,
My soul regained.

Though I have a pleasant wife
I'm the torment of her life,
Nerves I possess.
When I'm short of tobac'
Then of hell there's no lack,
And nothing less.

Ere I smoke, I am cross,
I am bound to be boss,
Of the whole machine,
Bound am I to be king,
And to power do I cling
Caring not for queen.

Ere I smoke in early morn
There's a fiend in me born
Ready for a muss.
Then my wife must beware
Of her tongue, or else there
Will be a fuss.

But when smoking I've begun
She her tongue can let run,
I'm but a lamb.
She can nose me all about,
Turn my pockets inside out,
For I feel so calm.

Thus it is in life's dream
That I drift down the stream,
Vile habit's slave.
All of us, who chew or smoke,
Have a fiend within our cloak,
And who can save?

THE GLORIOUS WEED.

TOBACCO is a Glorious Weed,
   Its praises we will sing,
To those, who lead a temperate life
The gauntlet we will fling;
The sage and the philosopher
Its virtues, they have tried:
It remedies all ills of life
Extending far and wide.
Then fill us up the old meerschaum,
And fill it to the brim,
And let us have a jolly, old smoke,
Before we tumble in.

With smoke ascending like a cloud,
Our souls it will inspire,
With courage, for all ills of life,
Whatever may transpire;
And, oh! it is so very hard
To bid the weed farewell,
So let our voices all unite
And make this chorus swell,

Then fill us up the old meerschaum,
And fill it to the brim;
And let us have a jolly, old smoke,
Before we tumble in.

DEPRESSION AND EXHILARATION.

ON yesterday, I felt as if the golden bowl was breaking,
    My hopes seemed dead, all pleasures fled,
And naught seemed worth the taking.
My sky was blue with leaden hue,
And every pain was double,
My past a curse, my future worse,
And life a hollow bubble.

To-day a glorious change has come, the
Shoots of joy are springing,
My heart is light, full of delight, the
Bells of hope are ringing.
My sky is bright, with sparkling light,
My pathway gemmed with flowers,
My past a dream, my future green,
Bedewed with golden showers.

40

LITTLE SISTER NELL.

I NEVER shall forget the day
That Sister Nell was born,
You see, I was the youngest then,
And that was just the corn.

They said my nose was out of joint,
I felt of it to see;
The baby I could be no more,
Oh! miserable me.

I thought that it was very strange,
For I believed the yarn,
That they had found her underneath
The floor of our old barn.

And after that, I often searched
Beneath that old barn floor, .
To see if I could not scare up
One or two sisters more.

Although they plagued me most to death,
I rather liked the style,
To have a sister of my own,
To have her all the while.

And that same day I brought her flowers
I thought she'd like to see,
But mother said, "She is too young,
Oh! what a boy you be."

I bragged among the other boys,
And cut an awful swell,
And told them I had got at home
A little Sister Nell.

But when she had some older grown
My living I did earn;

For then, I had to tote her round
In a four-wheeled concern.

I guess you'd think she liked to ride,
She never got enough,
And my poor legs, how they did ache,
It did seem rather rough.

And then I had to rock her crib
And tiresome vigils keep,
And oh! it always seemed to me
She'd never go to sleep.

And if I left her any time
To have a little play,
She'd make a fuss, and scream and yell,
The devil was to pay.

Then bursting in upon the scene
My mother, she would come,
And say, "You've 'bused poor 'ittle Nell,
I'll paddle you, my son."

And generally she kept her word,
I had the marks to show,
For when I went to sit me down
I had to go it slow.

Yet for all that, I know I liked
My little Sister Nell,
I think she hankered after me
And this she showed full well.

You see, she had a pretty face,
And pretty eyes and hair:
I guess I was some proud of her,
Oh! she was very fair.

And when I wished to stay from school
With other boys to play,
My mother said, "Yes, stay and tend
Your Sister Nell to-day."

Although the truth I would not own,
I rather liked to stay,
Though from the house I could not roam
With other boys to play.

I tell you what, we had great fun,
For Sister Nell was cute;
She pounded for me on the drum
While I did toot the flute.

Though a great racket we did make
I knew that all was well,

It was all right a noise to make
In tending Sister Nell.

And when the winter it had come,
I hauled her on my sled,
And tipped her off into a drift,
She went in heels o'er head.

My mother came and pulled her out,
A-gasping for her breath;
The look that mother gave to me,
It made me feel like death.

And when her breath came back again
She did not cry or roar,
But only said, "Mamma, I want
To go and 'ide some more."

But mother said, "Oh! no, you sha'n't,
He'll lose you in the snow,"
Then she began to yell and scream,
So mother let her go.

But now she's grown to womanhood,
And married, too, oh dear!
And when she plays and sings for me,
I almost seem to hear

The racket that we used to make
When she did pound the drum,
And I did toot on the old flute,
Oh! that was glorious fun.

And then it really seems to me
She's Little Nell again;
Sometimes, I almost seem to wish
That thus she could remain.

'Tis hard for me to bid adieu
To little Sister Nell,
For that she'll always be to me,
And that she knows full well.

May Heaven bless her, all her life,
And give her greatest joy,
A prayer that comes from out the heart
That loved her when a boy.

GO HAVE THE PHRENOLOGIST FEEL OF YOUR HEAD.

IF you have the desire to lead a good life,
　　Avoiding all quarrels, all discords, and strife,
And if you desire to be happy and wise,
In the battle of life, to win you a prize,

Put forth a great effort, and study yourself.
This course it will yield you both pleasure and pelf;
How to study yourself is easily said,
Go have the Phrenologist feel of your head.

If you desire to know each meanness, each trait,
That blackens your soul, both the little and great,
That drives you along to the greatest extremes,
Causing torments by day, and by night bad dreams;
If you wish to know how to hold these fiends down
Until they're your slaves and you wear victory's crown,
Very simple the task, and easily said,
Go have the Phrenologist feel of your head.

If your conduct in life runs in a wrong groove
And you wish to find out just how to improve
All the nobler feelings, that adorn your mind,
For in every one some good we can find;
If you wish to know all your beauties of soul,
And how to develop and perfect the whole,
The truth it is plain, and is easily said,
Go have the Phrenologist feel of your head.

If you wish to find out what business to learn,
For which you have talent, by which you can earn
Yourself a good living, and something besides
For a rainy day or whatever betides;
What you can do best, and what best suits your taste,
Your talent as well, useful time not to waste,
What business to learn, can be easily said,
Go have the Phrenologist feel of your head.

If you have the desire to select a good wife
To enliven your home, and to bless your life,
Whose character, temperament, hair, and whose eyes,
With your own in all things closely harmonize;
If already married, you've cast your lot,
And wish to live happy with her you have got,
To obtain your desire is easily said,
Go have the Phrenologist feel of her head.

If you desire to live to a good old age,
To perform a long time on the world's great stage,
To preserve your health, so that long you may last
Ere life and its pleasures and troubles are passed;
If you desire to know how long you may stay
Ere the angel of Death shall call you away,
If this you would know, it is easily said,
Go have the Phrenologist feel of your head.

BEAUTIFUL BIRDS.

BEAUTIFUL birds, they come in the Spring,
  Beautiful birds, they leave in the Fall,
Beautiful birds, we can hear them sing,
  Beautiful, beautiful, one and all.

Beautiful birds, do they come at night?
  Beautiful birds, do they come in the day?
Beautiful birds, though unknown their flight,
  Beautiful, beautiful, every way.

Warbling birds, the sweet nightingale,
  Warbling birds, the linnet and thrush,
Warbling birds, the finch and wagtail,
  Warbling, warbling, ne'er too much.

Warbling birds, of cardinal red,
  Warbling birds, of heavenly blue,
Warbling birds, with a crested head;
  Warbling, warbling, for me and you.

Caroling birds, the robin and lark,
   Caroling birds, the sparrow and wren,
Caroling birds, from dawn until dark;
   Caroling, caroling, all for men.

Architect birds, the skilled oriole.
   Architect birds, that construct a bower,
Architect birds, that dig like a mole.
   Architects, architects, strange their power.

Ravenous birds, the vulture and kite,
   Ravenous birds, the hawk and the owl,

Ravenous birds, in no songs delight,
   Ravenous, ravenous, fair or foul.

Ravenous birds, how they soar away,
   Ravenous birds, through the clouds they scud,
Ravenous birds, they pounce on their prey;
   Ravenous, ravenous, fierce for blood.

Clambering birds, the artful cuckoo,
   Clambering birds, the parrot that talks,
Clambering birds, all the long day through,
   Clambering, clambering, strange their walks.

Swift running birds, the giant ostrich,
   Swift running birds, they speed like the light,
Swift running birds, the great apteryx,
   Swift running, swift running, grand their flight.

Earth scratching birds, the domestic fowls,
   Earth scratching birds, the pheasant and quail,
Earth scratching birds, the guinea that howls;
   Earth scratching, earth scratching, at wholesale.

Stilt walking birds, that wade in the stream,
   Stilt walking birds, that dance in the gale,
Stilt walking birds, for all legs they seem.
   Stilt walking, stilt walking, crane and rail.

Aquatic birds, the gull and the auk,
   Aquatic birds, the eider and teal,
Aquatic birds, the goose with its squawk;
   Aquatic, aquatic, true and real.

Aquatic birds, that live in the sea,
   Aquatic birds, that sail o'er the land,
Aquatic birds, in great flocks agree;
   Aquatic, aquatic, joyous band.

Various birds, each made on a plan,
   Various birds, each for its own sphere,
Various birds, all useful to man;
   Various, various, they appear.

'TIS HARD TO PART.

'TIS hard to part from you, my love,
   Our hearts have beat together
Full many a month, without a thought
The silken cord to sever;
But now 'tis done, and we must part,
Our earnest love concealing,
With friendly grace, and not a trace
Our sentiments revealing.

Well, he is rich and jewels rare
Your graceful form will cover,
And flowers of ease will strew your path,
He is a wealthy lover:
But I am poor, now doubly poor,
And you my hopes in blasting
Have left a pain, that will remain
As long as hearts are lasting.

Why should I blame you for the act?
Your father and your mother
Have trained you well, have schooled your heart,
And stamped you for the other.

You say, 'twill take away their care
And set their star a-glowing,
If to fulfill, you have the will
Your hand for life bestowing.

To-morrow is your wedding day,
The guests are all invited,
Your fate is sealed, my hopes are dead,
And I am left benighted.
The orange wreath and bridal veil
Your graceful form adorning,
A beauteous cloud, to me your shroud,
And I am left in mourning.

You say you wish, that I shall go
And see you change your station,
Behold the dreadful funeral rites,
And give congratulation.
Good heavens! am I made of steel?
Can I choke down all feeling?
Will pride sustain the awful strain
That sets my brain a reeling?

Yes: I will go, since 'tis your will,
I'll smile, and laugh, and chatter,
I'll be a puppet in the show,
For what I feel, don't matter.

I'll say it is a splendid match
His wealth, your worth comparing,
They'll cut a dash and make a splash,
And set the world a staring.

The floor is ready for the ball,
The dancers are arraying,
The golden wheel has crushed the worm;
The band will soon be playing,
And many a heart will bound and thrill,
While feet the time are keeping,
I think perchance, I'll try the dance
While memory is sleeping.

But now, farewell, the game is played,
Good bye, good bye, forever,
Our paths diverge, our Spring has fled,
And now comes wintry weather;
In fancy now I seem to hear
The wedding bells a-pealing,
And every bell strikes forth a knell
Your hollow heart revealing.

TO ALICE.

IN friendship's bands we are entwined,
   I can forget you never,
We're bound on earth by holy ties
   That naught but death can sever.

And as the years pass slowly by,
   Let these words be a token
Of the friendship true, I bear for you,
   That never can be broken.

AWAKEN MY LOVE.

AWAKEN my love, my joy, and my life,
    The light of my eyes, my dear little wife;
You twine round my heart like a tender vine,
And you fill my soul with your love divine.
When I think of you, how my pulses thrill,
And my blood, it bounds like a rushing rill
Through my heart and brain, and my soul is stirred
By the sweetest strains that mortals have heard;
The music of love is thrilling my heart,
There let it remain, and never depart.

Although others may not think you so fair,
To me, you are beautiful everywhere.
My fancy paints you with many a grace,
With a willowy form, and soul-lit face,
With such shapely feet, that their queenly tread
Methinks, I could hear though my form were dead;
Whose elastic step my spirit would hear
And thrill with delight, when you came me near.
And your slender hand as it smoothes my brow
Is a balm to my soul, I feel it now;

When tired and weary with daily strife
It rouses my soul and gives me new life;
What a wondrous power, that magical hand,
It seems like a gift from the fairy land;
When I clasp it in mine, 'tis joy to my heart,
There let it remain, and never depart.

Your face is a world of beauty to me,
Its many glories, in fancy, I see,
There are gems of pearl, in a rose-bud mouth,
And lips, unrivaled in the North or South
For delicate sweetness, whose touch would thrill,
And the wave of pleasure my breast would fill;
And my soul would soar to regions of bliss
On the wings of that pure angelic kiss;
When those lips touch mine, such feelings arise
That they open the gates of Paradise.
Your last kiss of love is yet in my heart,
There let it remain, and never depart.

I love every feature of your sweet face,
Each one is a type of beauty and grace;
There is a neck like the snow, a dimpled cheek,
A symmetrical chin, and eyes that speak
Of a power to feel the keenest joy,
The highest of pleasure without alloy;

Of a power to suffer the worst of pain
That ever tormented the heart or brain;
A power to hate, and power to love,
To love like an angel from heaven above,
To love with a zeal that can never tire,
With undying strength that will never expire,
To love, just as long as your life shall last,
To love, when your life with its trials are past:
All this vast wealth of love on me you shower,
Your heart is my rose, my beautiful flower.
Whose fragrance of love all my senses fill
With untold delight, and I feel it still,
Though from your dear presence I'm far away,
That fragrance is here, I sense it to-day,
And I feel it rush down deep in my heart,
There let it remain, and never depart.

I'M COMING TO MEET YOU, MY PET.

IT was hard to leave you, my Pet,
   For you seemed a part of my life,
That parting, I ne'er shall forget,
   My own darling, precious, my wife.
My foolish heart trembled with fear
   As I kissed your sweet lips o'er and o'er,
That something might happen, my dear,
   That would cause us to meet never more.

I'm coming to meet you, my Pet,
   I'll take your sweet hand in my own,
And then, I will never regret
   The time, which in absence has flown;
I'll press your sweet form to my breast,
   And feel your heart beat against mine,
And then, will my soul be at rest,
   And revel in pleasure divine.

I will press your sweet lips to mine,
   I will feel the ecstatic bliss,
That nothing could tempt to resign
   As I steal from them kiss after kiss.

I will wrap you in an embrace
    That will fill our hearts with delight,
The love-light will beam on my face,
    And naught will our happiness blight.

Our forms will entwine like two vines
    And form a most beautiful wreath,
Our spirits will mingle like wines
    And we'll float on the river of Lethe.

And time will flow on in its flight
  As we float on the golden tide,
Each moment a pearl of delight,
  My own darling, precious, my bride.

You will feel that I am your king,
  I will feel that you are my queen,
And each to the other will bring
  Perennial joys, ever green.
And our bark will sail on the stream,
  The beautiful river of Lethe;
And our life, a heavenly dream,
  Untroubled by sorrow or grief.

But the river of Lethe, my dear,
  Flows into the river of death,
And when its dark waters appear.
  O'er its surface we'll glide like a breath.
When we've passed to the other side
  We'll enter the river of life,
And then you will still be my bride,
  My darling, sweet, precious, my wife.

And if we are nothing but earth,
  Our ashes will mingle, my dear,
And when they receive the new birth,
  Side by side, in a wreathe we'll appear;

Together we'll pass through the gate
  Of that glorious city above.
Although changed from this earthly state
  We will always continue to love.

I am coming to meet you, my Pet,
  And soon we shall both see the light
Of a sun that is never to set
  On two hearts that are filled with delight.
You are waiting to greet me, my love,
  You tremble to think I am near,
My darling, my beautiful dove,
  I'm coming, behold me! I'm here.

THE FALSE-HEARTED WIDOW.

DOES your memory ever wander
    Back to scenes of long ago,
When our lives were bright with sunshine,
Ere our locks were tinged with snow?
Does your memory tell the story,
How my heart with love you fired,
By your womanly caresses,
By your touch and voice inspired?

How you lured me on and onward,
Till my soul was all aglow
With the fire that burned within me;
And my blood rushed to and fro
Through the channels of my nature,
Like a mighty mountain stream,
Boiling, surging, with emotion,
Surely, 'twas no idle dream.

Ah! distinctly I remember,
'Twas a dreary winter's night,
And the wind moaned o'er the house-tops
And the ground was robed in white,

5   65

But within the fire burned brightly
And the room was all aglow,
As we sat alone together,
On that night so long ago.

You were many years the older,
You a widow, I a youth,
And it seems you were the bolder,
Surely I must tell the truth —
You before, the ropes had handled,
Ah! too well you knew your part,
'Twas but child's play for your fancy
To entrap a youthful heart.

Suddenly you rose up, starting,
Came to where I was reclined,
Drooped your willowy form above me,
And with lips that velvet lined,
Touched my brow, with gentle pressure,
Thrilled my heart with unknown bliss,
Filled my soul with untold rapture,
O, the magic of that kiss!

Then your queenly head drooped lower,
Till it laid upon my breast,
And you seemed a placid infant
That had sweetly sank to rest;

"THEN CAME KISSES, HOT AND BURNING,
MINGLED IN WITH WARM EMBRACES."

Then we formed an artist's picture
As our hearts, beat side by side,
Then and there, our troth was plighted,
And you swore to be my bride.

Swore we by the stars in heaven,
By that God we both adored,
To be faithful to each other;
And upon love's altar poured
Finest feelings of our nature.
All the room seemed filled with light,
Unseen angels seemed to hover,
All around us, on that night.

Then came words of tender accent,
Then came scarlet blushing faces,
Then came kisses, hot and burning,
Mingled in with warm embraces;
Then the bell tolled for retiring,
Then we parted at your door.
Would to God that we had parted
On that night for evermore.

Days and weeks, we spent in wooing,
Days, I never shall forget,
O, that blissful, happy, season,
Burns within my memory yet.

O! to think that you could wound me,
That you could play such a part,
That beneath your form of beauty
Lay a false, deceitful heart.

But the time soon came for parting,
And to battle with the world,
I went forth a youthful stranger,
And into the contest hurled
All the powers of my nature;
How I worked by day and night,
Knowing if I was successful
We could very soon unite.

In my absence came another,
He was richer far than I,
On his wealth and his position
You soon turned an eager eye;
And to him, your troth you plighted,
And to me you broke your vow,
For I was your idle plaything,
But I can forgive you now.

For as years have on me gathered
I have somewhat wiser grown,
And the glamour of your beauty
From my unchained heart has flown.

Now I see your inward nature
Was an image of deceit,
Lacking all the nobler virtues
And your life was all a cheat.

And I often shrink and shudder,
Shrink and shudder, as I think
Of how near I came to wed you,
Ere I halted on the brink.
Yes! O freely, I forgive you,
And bless him, who took my place,
For poor martyr, he has saved me
From a lifetime of disgrace.

THE METAMORPHOSIS OF A BUTTERFLY.

A T first, 'twas an egg on the branch of a tree,
  So small and minute, that the eye could scarce see
Or outline its form, yet, in its tiny shell
Was a germ of life, all contained in one cell,

Which favored by warmth, by the air, and the light,
Soon turns to a worm and bursts forth into sight,
A caterpillar, with a marvelous form,
All bristling with hairs, to protect and to warm,
Having compound eyes, and formidable jaws,
Many pairs of legs, and some, armed with claws;

A stomach, with power to digest and to grind
The food that it eats when such food it can find.
Each joint of its form has a great central nerve,
Blood vessels, and lungs, its own purpose to serve:
Forty thousand muscles, make up its plan,
There are less than five hundred found in a man;
Its mouth and front legs form a spinning machine,
The most wonderful loom that ever was seen,
For the finest of silks, it spins and it weaves
From substances gathered from out of the leaves.

Indeed, it is strange, that an egg so minute,
Such a curious form, could thus evolute,
But nature is full of mysterious things,
And many strange facts to observers she brings.
Soon after its birth, in that queer larval state,
It travels along at a very slow rate
In quest of its food, and it soon finds a leaf
Which it swiftly devours affording relief.
'Tis the greatest glutton that ever was seen,
In fact, 'tis a powerful eating machine,
Just think of a man of such gastric powers,
Who eats twice his weight every twenty-four hours;
If he weighed two hundred, one fifth of a ton
Every day in the week, down his throat would run,
But the caterpillar, I desire to state,
Gulps down every day more than twice his own weight.

Far too large for his skin, his body soon grows
He casts it aside like a suit of old clothes,
Four times in his life does he cast off his skin,
I'll tell you the truth, though you may think it *thin.*

The next change that occurs, I now will relate,
For the larva, now enters the pupal state,
It entwines round its body a silken fold
And takes a long sleep like Van Winkle of old:
Now during this sleep many changes take place,
It loses some legs, and obtains a new face,
In its dreams, pass away its numerous claws,
Its vermiform shape, and its powerful jaws.

Rainbow-tinted wings on its body appear,
And develop, in beauty, the eye to cheer,
This great transformation is finished at last
And the caterpillar is a thing of the past.
Soon it works its way out of its silken tomb,
Unfolds its bright wings, which for flight it does plume,
And then flits away among blossoms and flowers,
Idly sipping their sweets, thus passing the hours,
It leads a gay life, though it soon passes by,
This radiant creature, this bright butterfly,
No more to devour the green pulp of the leaves,
For its spinning has ceased and no more it weaves.

TRANSFORMATION OF THE TADPOLE.

A TADPOLE was born from the egg of a frog,
His home was a pool, far down in a bog,
And some people called him a polliwog;
Like a fish, he'd gills the water to breathe;
Like a fish, through the water he could cleave;
Like a fish, he'd little his soul to grieve.

But this naughty tadpole was not content,
To be like a fish was not his intent,
And this he asserted wherever he went:
He saw grass and rushes bordering his pool,
And land beyond, looking shady and cool,
Says he, "Ill explore it, and be no fool."

But to explore the land he must have feet
To walk or to jump on, his wants to meet,
And lungs to breathe air, perfect and complete.
To Nature he came with his strange request;
She granted his wish, set his heart at rest;
With both lungs and legs the tadpole was blest.

He soon found his gills beginning to fail,
And a strange shrinkuption attacked his tail,
While lungs grew in him, like those of a whale;
And he also found, to his great surprise,
His mouth widening out to a barn-door size,
While legs from his body began to rise.

The hindermost pair, they grew very fast;
Both tail and gills became things of the past:
The strange transformation was done at last.
Then, swimming close to the edge of the bog,
He leaped on the land, a wonderful frog,
Never more to be called a polliwog.

He' could travel on land, in water dive,
As quick as a flash could catch flies alive;
On this kind of diet he seemed to thrive.
Now this frog was gifted with powers of song;
Far into the night his notes he'd prolong;
His voice it was *bass*, and extremely strong.

I heard him one night, at the edge of the bog,
Singing his lay, as he sat on a log,
And this was his song — The Tale of the Frog.

THE TALE OF THE FROG.

Come, all frogs and froglings, listen to me,
While I tell the tale of our ancestry,
And you'll find it noble a frog to be:
For the frog that takes no pride in his birth
Is worse than a tadpole, not fit for earth;
But of such low frogs there is a great dearth.

Since our ancestors' birth, a billion years
Have cycled away, and yet it appears
That we still inhabit this vale of tears.
Our ancestors came from far down the scale,
From Ascidians, without head or tail,
Who were spliced together as long as a rail.

'Tis a fact, which modern science has shown,
That one branch of these evolved a backbone,
Or something, from which vertebrates have grown.
From the lowest of these came the polliwog,
Which in progression still onward did jog
Until it developed into the frog.

In the Trias system, ages ago,
Our forefathers lived and danced to and fro,
Leaving their bones and their footprints to show.
In the Triassic system we can trace
The fossil remains of a giant race,
That flourished not far from this very place.

There was one whose foot, when spread on a log,
Took ten times the room of a modern frog,
And fifty times that of a polliwog;
He possessed a vast form to gaze upon;
He bore the long name Labyrinthodon,
And his weight came very close to a ton.

And his voice, good heavens! all language will fail,
To describe its power in my simple tale—
'Twas a cannon's roar, the snore of a whale.
Another great frog, that thought he was some,
Whose tracks were called Cheirotherium,
But all of these giants their race have run.

In the carbon age, when ferns were great trees,
Also mosses, cat-tails, and, besides these,
Stigilarian forests waved in the breeze,
Trees that would have made gigantic saw-logs,
And under them lived the primeval frogs,
Great creatures with tails then played in the bogs.

From what I have said you can plainly see
Though now tied to earth, we had great ancestry,
Although smaller now than we used to be.
Some of our past species have learned to fly,
Developing wings, they soared through the sky;
We frogs are the tailings of days gone by.

We spend too much time in fooling around,
In sparking and dancing over the ground,
In hunting for mates that cannot be found;
We always are looking up to the sky;
We can only leap, and we ought to fly;
When I think of all this, it makes me sigh.

Now if to improve we have the desire,
For a pair of wings let each frog aspire,
And call on Nature to make him a flyer;
For what has been done in the ages passed,
May be done again if we only hold fast,
For this state of things cannot always last.

When our wings have grown, what a splendid thing,
No more will we catch insects with a spring,
But we'll gobble them down while on the wing.
I am growing hoarse, and must end my song,
For I fear I've detained you much too long,
All join in this chorus and make it strong.

CHORUS OF THE FROGS.

We hop and we skip all over the logs,
We sing and we dance all among the bogs,
In the pools we visit the polliwogs,
We're progressing upward with steady jogs,
We're a happy, rollicking set of frogs.

THE SCIENCE OF MAN: AN OUTLINE OF PHRENOLOGY.

ALL nature is truth, above and below.
    Beside and around, wherever we go;
Though nature is truth, all men have not read
Her beautiful leaves so lavishly spread:
We open her book. the chapter is man:
We read he is made on a certain plan;
Then casting our eyes a little below,
We see these plain words, the head, it will show.

To prove this great truth, a fact I will cite,
You never can find two heads just alike,
Go ask of nature, and search through her plan
From the lowest snail to the highest man,
You will find no two, in each tribe or race,
Have just the same shape of head or of face.
All natures differ, some more, and some less,
The forms of the head, all the shades express:

The idiot has such a little head
There's no room for brains, and his mind is dead.
The Australian savage is still alive.
Whose head is small, and he cannot count five.

Why the poor negro does not more attain
Is stamped by nature upon his small brain.
The Caucasian makes far greater progress;
The negro of brain, has ten ounces less.

THE SIZE AND QUALITY OF THE BRAIN AS INDICATIVE OF MENTAL POWER.

The chapter is man, this great truth we find
That the brain is the organ of the mind,
Another great truth is proved every hour,
The size of the brain indicates its power:
That is, if quality, texture of hair,
Fineness or coarseness of brain we compare;
The man of coarse brain has a sluggish mind,
Though a mammoth head on his trunk we find,
He ne'er may expect the great world to rule,
For a Webster's head is oft placed on a fool.

The man of fine brain, though small be his head,
Has an active mind, is shrewd and well read,
In business may thrive, in science and art,
And in society play well his part.
Of course he's not great, his medium brain
Cannot soar far above the common plain,
And yet, he may be a popular man
And serve a good end in the world's great plan,

But greatness requires a much larger brain
To soar far above the world's common plain,
Not only larger, but of finer clay,
And well balanced, too, that its parts may play
Harmoniously like men, that well drilled
Each knowing his place and each place well filled.

NAPOLEON,

It has been written by history's pen
That of largest brain are the greatest men:
Alexander's head was of a great size,
He conquered the world, it became his prize;
Napoleon, too, had a giant head,
And kingdoms crashed down at his stately tread;

6

GEORGE WASHINGTON.

And Washington was to victory led
By a brain well balanced, in a large head.

Earth's greatest orators large heads can show,
Demosthenes, Antony, and Cicero.
In modern times we have Webster and Clay,
While John P. Irish is living to-day;
If this great orator you chance to hear,
While his eloquence flows, so smooth and clear,
Just mark his head, its fine shape and large size,
His fullness of brow, his prominent eyes,
Then if in science of man you are read
You can see *his* power is shown by his head.

The great poets, too, who sweetest have sung,
Homer and Virgil, Pope, Dryden and Young,
And many others, whose fancies did soar,
Such as Byron and Burns, Milton and Moore,
All had good sized heads and brains that were fine;
While Shakspeare stands at the head of the line.
Just note his picture, gaze on his great brow,
The king of poets is before you now.
And yet, there is one, though unknown to fame,
But modesty says, "O breathe not his name!"

Great scientists, too, have had heavy brains,
Which last have been weighed with very much pains.

The first, on whom my memory pounces,
Is Cuvier's, which weighed sixty-four ounces.
While Doctor Dupuytren and Abercrombie,
Pulled down on the scale about sixty-three,
The average man's brain weighs but forty-nine,
But greatness, it soars far above this line;
Of idiots born, there are a great plenty,
Whose average brains weigh less than twenty.
Place all the great men in a single row
And a glance will prove that their heads do show.

GENIUS EXPLAINED.

This fact, we observe in our life's great school,
That genius oft lives in the head of a fool.
By genius, we mean, that strange power of mind,
Which untaught, does things to astonish mankind.
Please notice this fact. which we have to tell,
A genius can do only one thing well;
In all other respects you'll find him weak.
For other great talents you need not seek.
His whole brain and mind all go to one thing,
To develop that. his nature did bring
All of the strength that in him it could find,
Robbing all other parts of brain and mind:
In this way is formed a being unequal.
A genius is born. and he is the sequel.

Who can play his part, and play it so well,
That no other human can him excel.

To illustrate this I will only quote
Of Blind Tom, who is a genius of note,
Who has the great gift, though strange it appears,
To imitate all the sounds that he hears;
To reproduce them so perfect and clear,
That the self-same notes fall again on the ear;
And thus does he play his unstudied part,
A perfect mimic of nature and art.
He is the most perfect sounding machine
That the ear has heard or the eye has seen,
Yet, in moulding his brain on the sounding plan,
Nature spoiled all the nobler parts of the man:
Thus giving the world a genius, a fool,
Who sits on a throne and a dunce's stool.

Another great genius Missouri yields,
Who goes by the name of Reuben Fields—
A mathematical prodigy, who
The most intricate problem can go through
So quickly, that there seems no time between
The statement and answer to intervene.
I've met him myself, and therefore can state
That he uses neither pencil nor slate,

But solves all the problems in his own mind,
To the great surprise of all human kind.
If you tell him your age at night or morn,
He'll tell what day of the week you were born,
And in the next breath, ere you could count five,
The number of seconds you've been alive;
He carries no watch, for that would not pay,
His mind keeps the time by night and by day;
He can tell the changes of moon and sun
For a million years that are yet to come;
And if you think he is going too fast,
He will date all the changes of the past.
He's a human clock with almanac traits;
A figuring machine and a stack of dates;
In fact, his whole mind all runs to figures,
As some politician's does to niggers.
And yet he never attended a school,
While outside of figures he's naught but a fool —
Another sample of Nature's strange plan,
Both genius and idiot all in one man.

From this we must not imply, as a rule,
That each man of talent must needs be a fool;
No one would a fool for a great man take,
Yet fools great geniuses often make.
The truly great man has a balanced brain,
With a few strong points, and yet, in the main,

No part that goes to the greatest excess,
But each part is developed more or less.
With the genius this is seldom the case,
He is the extremes of the human race.
Now if we observe this truth we will know
That all human talents the head will show.

THE TEMPERAMENTS DEFINED.

The next thing in order we now present,
Is an important theme — the temperament;
To man's physical nature it does relate,
His structure, formation, condition or state.
The term temperament may be well defined
As a form of body that acts on the mind,
Causing different actions, manners and ways;
For temperament the bias of mind portrays.

THE VITAL OR SANGUINE TEMPERAMENT.

With three systems of organs man is blessed,
And first the Vital occupies the chest,
Giving its owner a very full form,
With plenty of blood to keep him warm;
A florid complexion, blue eyes, brown hair,
And full cheeks, and lips with these to compare:
This form of the body does represent
The Vital or Sanguine Temperament.

Full of bounding blood are men of this form,
Joyous and happy, gay, ardent and warm;
For they always look on the brightest side,
On the wings of hope does their spirits ride;
They are full of steam, and they charge about
To the right and left with many a shout;
They love to be boss, and see others work,
But when there's hard digging they always shirk;
Yet they never get tired of sport or play —
They can freeze to that all the livelong day.
In reading they do not take much delight,
Unless it is something that's very light;
They always desire to see any show,
Are fond of talking, and great on the blow;
Are quite freehearted and willing to give,
They have the desire to let others live:
Have great enterprise, are always alive;
When they live in a town, business must thrive.
They always are going to do a big thing,
Into all speculations their stamps they fling;
All during their lives their flags are unfurled,
They move the great wheels of the business world.

If your wife of this form happens to be,
Brown haired and blue eyed, or a blonde is she —
The prettiest women that eyes have seen
Of the Sanguine Temperament ever have been —

She smiles quite often, but seldom does frown,
You're the happiest man in all the town;
She likes to board, and all labor will shirk,
But hire her a girl and she'll boss the work.
Yet altogether she makes a good wife,
A sweet companion that blesses your life.

THE LYMPHATIC TEMPERAMENT.

If diseased, the Sanguine may represent
A form called the Lymphatic Temperament.
Such men on the gooseberry plan are made,
With great mountains of fat around them laid.
They eat too much for the labor they do,
And they laze around all the long year through,
They're shiftless and stupid, fond of their ease,
But with plenty to eat, they're not hard to please.

THE MOTIVE OR BILIOUS TEMPERAMENT.

The bones and the muscles, they represent
The Motive or Bilious Temperament,
Which constitutes men with angular forms,
Long feet and long legs, long hands and long arms,
Long bodies, long necks, long noses, and all
Which combined render them extremely tall;
With hair dark and coarse, and eyes deeply set,
Their slab-sided, lank forms, needing flesh to get.
As boys, they are always awkward and green,

THE MOTIVE TEMPERAMENT.

Overgrown, for all legs and arms they seem,
It takes a long time for them to mature,
And like a draft horse, they are slow but sure.
As men, they possess a great deal of grit
And will not back down, not even a whit,
And when they've once put their hand to the plow,
They're bound to go through if it takes a cow.
If they are your friends, they will love you well,
But their hate is like the essence of Hell;
For all of earth's labors, such men are good,
The drawers of water and hewers of wood.

If your wife has this form she never flirts,
The buttons are always sewed on your shirts,
All work of the household is neatly done
From earliest morn to the set of sun,
But beware, and never tempt her to scold,
Or the grave will claim you ere you are old.

THE BILIOUS-NERVOUS TEMPERAMENT.

If slender the form, with dark hair and eyes,
The texture is fine, and moderate the size,
The Bilious-Nervous this form represents,
Which is one of the finest temperaments;
It combines mental strength with physical powers,
In such minds oft blossom ambitious flowers,

OLIVER CROMWELL.

ANDREW JACKSON.

CAESAR THE GREAT.

To illustrate this three names I will state,
They are Jackson, Cromwell and Cæsar the Great.

BILIOUS-SANGUINE TEMPERAMENT.

If the hair be dark, and dark be the eyes,
And fleshy the form, of good breadth and size,
The Bilious-Sanguine this does represent,
Which is an extremely good temperament,
Combining ardor, with physical strength,
Which oft prolongs life to an extreme length.
Men of this form can work or take their ease,
In either position not hard to please.
When they work, for no man will they give down.
When idle, the laziest men in town:
Taking all in all, this form it is fine,
For success and pleasure, it does combine.

THE MENTAL OR NERVOUS TEMPERAMENT.

The whole nervous system does represent
The Nervous or Mental Temperament.
When the brain and the nerves predominate,
Then this form of body it does create,
The head is large, and the body is small,
The form is slender, whether short or tall,
The hair is fine, the complexion is light,
And the eyes are gray, with a sparkling light,

The features are sharp, and the voice is high,
While all of the motions are quick and spry,
The men of this form all like mental work,
But all other kinds of labor they shirk;
They're fond of study, of nature and art,
In literature they play well their part;

Mrs. ANNA H. JUDSON,
The Mental Temperament.

All artists and poets that mankind bless
Possess of this temperament more or less;
Such men use their brains and minds much too fast
And the mental machine wears out at last;

They are brilliant, and swift does rise their sun,
But it sets ere half of their day is done,
Their life it is short, but a fleeting breath,
Which is soon eclipsed by the pall of death.

All men of this form have far too much brain
For the blood of their bodies to sustain.
'Tis the steam that makes the great engine go,
And blood is the steam of the brain we know.
No thoughts or ideas can mind maintain
Without the heart forces blood to the brain:
Cut off the supply, and quickly we find
All action to cease in the human mind;
If on a weak form a large brain is seen
'Tis like a large mill on a limited stream:
Though the mill be fine, the machinery good,
'Tis in the wrong place, it lacks the life blood.
And thus, as a rule, we usually find
Weakness of body with weakness of mind.

The greatest of men have not only large brains,
But strong constitutions and iron frames.
Examine earth's heroes and then we find
The physical giants of all mankind:
Daniel Webster possessed a mammoth brain
And a powerful body, did it sustain.

He was forty-four inches around the chest,
And great was the strength his body possessed.
Another great light, to his country a sun,

DANIEL WEBSTER.

How familiar his name, George Washington.
Who was noted for strength while yet a boy,
Great bodily vigor did he enjoy:

7

What a splendid form, what a well-knit frame,
What a powerful brain, it did sustain.

To this rule, but few exceptions we find,
And in most of these, the ambitious mind
Wears out the body thus stopping the work,
Cutting off the life with a sudden jerk.
Prince William of Orange possessed a weak frame
And an ambitious mind, that aspired to fame,
Though his feeble frame kept holding him back,
He persevered, nor would take the back track,
Though brought to his bed oft by sickness and pain,
He was always up and at it again.
Thus years passed away, and when the first beam
Of his rising sun was beginning to gleam,
Which was to repay him for all of those years
Of toils and of pains, of hopes and of fears,
His body gave out and down shot his sun,
But the beam remained of all he had done
What he might have been, cannot be defined,
Had a stronger body sustained his mind;
Now if we but glance his history o'er,
'Tis easily seen, he'd have done much more,
And thus, as a rule, we usually find
That a weak body will vanquish the mind.

It is the Nervous Temperament
That large brains with weak frames does represent.
Such should develop their physical powers
By exercise, healthful at proper hours,
They should breathe an abundance of heaven's pure air,
And should manage their diet with greatest care;
They should try to increase their strength and size,
And if they succeed they win a great prize,
More precious, by far, than gold that's refined,
A body that balances, brain and mind.
But the trouble is they're sedentary
And stay in-doors like a caged canary;
Not all are nervous, and yet they have nerves,
Which they manifest when occasion serves.
All are excitable and when in a hurry
They usually are in an awful flurry;
They are always afraid that they will be late,
Are often too early, and have to wait,
If any misfortune happens to burst
They see the worst side from the very first,
And suffer intensely at what does befall,
And afterward find it was nothing at all.
When they enjoy, their enjoyment is great,
They laugh and they joke at a breakneck rate,
But when they suffer, they turn to the wall,
And in life, they can see no pleasure at all.

One moment their hearts with pleasure will swell,
And the next, will be plunged in misery's hell,
They always go to the greatest extremes,
Are full of odd fancies, notions and dreams.
If your wife of this form happens to be,
A woman of many fine parts is she;
A woman of taste, a woman of mind,
A woman whose nature is much refined,
A woman of soul, a woman of sense,
A woman that is quite an expense,
A woman of style, a woman of pride,
A woman who's not to fashion tied,
A woman who shrinks from the gaping crowd,
A woman whose neighbors all praise aloud,
A woman with whom it is pleasant to dwell,
Unless she determines to make home a hell;
A woman whom no man can easily rule,
A woman, in fact, who is nobody's fool;
For she can be pleasant, and smooth, and slick,
And at the same time cut you to the quick.
Each little mean thing you've done in your life
Will be treasured up by your darling wife;
And when she is vexed, be it less or more,
On your devoted head the dose she'll pour;
And you often lose your own self-respect,
For you never can tell just what to expect;

If you treat her well, then happy your life,
She'll make you more than an average wife;
If you treat her ill, you had better roam,
For you'll have a fiend to sweeten your home.

NEWTON.
WELL-BALANCED TEMPERAMENT.

A well-balanced temperament is the best
With which a woman or man can be blest;
For the Motive, Mental and Vital blend,
And to a most perfect harmony tend;

The Motive gives strength and power to endure,
The Mental great powers of mind insure,
While the Vital furnishes all the steam
That nature requires to run the machine.

MADAME De STAEL.
WELL-BALANCED TEMPERAMENT.

Of this well-balanced form has ever been
The finest examples of women and men;
We will name but two, fame has told their tale,
Sir Isaac Newton and Madame de Stael.

ANALYSIS OF THE MENTAL FACULTIES.

Now when one examines this mind of ours
We find it is formed of two kinds of powers—
First, the Feelings, which sense, pleasure and pain,
And which inhabit that part of the brain
Which always is covered by flowing hair,
Except in bald persons whose polls are bare.
Second, the Intellect, which all directs,
Remembers, contrives, invents and reflects,
All of whose organs inhabit a bed
Above the eyes in the human forehead;
Thus many faculties make up the mind,
And each has a special function, we find;
Each has its part of the mind to sustain,
And each is expressed by a part of the brain,
Or each faculty has one part of the brain
Through which it acts, called an organ by name—
Both organ and faculty mean the same,
And therefore both possess the same name.
Three classes of organs were made for all,
The Social, the Selfish and the Moral.

THE SOCIAL FEELINGS.

The Social Feelings by which men are led
Occupy the lower back part of the head;
They socialize man, give him the desire
For marriage and friends, and his own hearth-fire;

First, *Amativeness* does our souls perplex,
And we fall in love with the other sex;
And soon we marry a husband or wife;
Conjugality says be true for life,
For if you are ever to me untrue,
I'll jealous become and raise hell with you.
And soon little children come to the nest,
And then our *Parental Love* is blest;
How happy we feel as we dance on our knee
The babe that a president is to be.
To enjoy this life we all must have friends,
And *Adhesiveness* to that business attends.
To be happy we must not always roam,
Inhabitativeness gives the love of home.
To succeed, our thoughts must adhere to each plan,
Concentrativeness gives this power to man.
And thus we have, as here truly defined,
All the social virtues that gem the mind.

THE SELFISH FEELINGS.

Self-preservation is nature's first law,
Throughout animal life this rule has no flaw;
The selfish group, in this beautiful plan,
Are for the self-preservation of man.
They guard all his interests with jealous care,
Of danger and death teach him to beware,

Give him industry that he may not want,
Spirit and courage that nothing can daunt;
All good in themselves, when properly used,
But leading to evils when they're abused;
For when perverted or in great excess,
They make man a demon and nothing less.
All the selfish organs near the ears are found,
On the sides of the head, above and around.

We all wish to live in this world of strife—
Vitativeness gives us the love of life;
If all men were cowards then beasts would be kings,
But *Combatative* courage prevents such things.
The pain of toothache often makes us yell,
But *Destructiveness* pulls it, and we are well.
When hungry a square meal always tastes good—
Alimentiveness gives the love of food.
There is one investment we know will pay,
To lay something by for a rainy day,
For we cannot always count on our health—
Acquisitiveness gives the desire for wealth.
All thoughts that we think will not do to tell—
Frankness is a gem but too much is not well;
This world we live in is matter-of-fact,
To get along well we must use some tact;
If you tell all you know you'll have none to tell,
Secretiveness says, hold your tongue a spell.

Perils surround us if danger we scorn,
Caution is watchful and ready to warn.
Thus the Selfish group, with exceptions none,
Cause man to look out for A Number One.

THE ASPIRING SENTIMENTS.

The Aspiring organs are located
In the upper and back part of the head,
That part which is usually called the crown;
They give man his love of fame and renown.
For earth's great places they give the desire,
And kindle the heart with ambitious fire.
They give man dignity, firmness and pride,
Vanity, conceit, and a hobby to ride.
I know that we all have peculiar ways,
And we all are more or less fond of praise;
Some like it well spread, others like it thin,
But every poor human will take some in;
Approbativeness gives the love of praise,
And makes us attend to what the world says;
In many this feeling runs to excess,
And they become slaves to fashion and dress.
When world upon world we compare with man
He seems but an atom in nature's plan;
Were it not for his pride he would feel quite small.
But *Self-esteem* says, you are greatest of all;

In the animal world you have no peer,
Be content with your lot and have no fear.

Though oft discouraged, we still persevere,
When but little hope our spirits can cheer,
For *Firmness* says, keep a stiff upper lip
And never say die, you'll yet save the ship.
Approbativeness, Firmness and Self-esteem,
The selfish sentiments, as we have seen,
In human character form a great part,
And success without them would soon depart.

THE MORAL SENTIMENTS.

The Moral feelings, whose organs are spread
Out in the uppermost part of the head,
Give man all his sense of justice and right,
All hopes that the fancy pictures so bright;
His reverence and faith in his Father above,
And last, but not least, Samaritan love.

First, *Conscientiousness* leads the van,
It offers the Golden Rule to man,
And strongly impels to justice and right;
Obeying this feeling makes the heart light;
But disobedience makes conscience frown,
And then with remorse the heart is weighed down.

Next, *Hope* in the heart gently comes to sing
Its beauteous song of Perennial Spring,
For each disappointment, that weighs us down,
It paints in the future a golden crown;
Hope is not content with the things of earth,
But looks far beyond to a heavenly birth;
And if there's no Heaven, in the world's great plan,
Then why was this feeling stamped upon man?

Next, *Spirituality* takes its place,
With all wonders and marvels it keeps its pace,
Giving faith in things seen and things unseen,
In what is to-day, and in what has been,
In what is present and what is to come,
In all things old or new under the sun.
Giving faith in God, giving faith in man,
Giving faith in everything that it can.
Veneration next in the soul takes its stand,
And high up toward Heaven it raises its hand;
It causes the savage to bend the knee
To the sun or moon, to a stone or tree,
Which, to him, are symbols of that great Hand,
Whose mighty power he cannot understand:
This feeling also with great strength applies
To things that are old, which it greatly does prize,
Old fashions, old customs, old fossils, old coins,
And all things which from the past it purloins.

Benevolence next falls into the line.
Her sweet face, with kindness and mercy shine,
O'er all of the frailties that cause human woes
Her mantle of charity gently she throws.
Her heart is so deep, so broad and so wide,
That it takes in all creatures on every side,
The poorest and meanest, as well as the best,
All in her great heart are taken to rest,
She causes husbands and wives to beware
And of all harsh actions to have a care,
She is the greatest gift, to mortals, given,
Wherever she dwells, her home is Heaven.

The moral feelings, which bless mankind,
Should always control the whole human mind,
Their organs were placed in the human brain
Man's animal nature to restrain:
These moral organs all brutes are without,
The line of division is here laid out
Between man and animals, written plain
By the Creator's hand, on the human brain;
But some men's brains from the very start
Are sadly lacking in the moral part;
Though their number is small, we cannot dispute
That each one of them is simply a brute.
But most of men when the light they first see
Have moral germs in a certain degree,

And if rightly trained, at school and at home,
Honest and virtuous they may become,
But if wrongly trained, and bad be their school,
The animal feelings their lives will rule,
The world will see only baser powers,
Nor catch the perfume of the moral flowers
That would have bloomed, but were nipped in the bud
And trampled to death in vice's foul mud.

THE SELF—PERFECTING FACULTIES.

Man loves the beautiful, grand and sublime,
To attain this he wanders through every clime;
O'er Tropical deserts of arid heat,
In Arctic regions, where the icebergs meet:
This love of beauty, in nature and art,
Of man's composition forms no small part:
To gratify this, Dame Nature her bed
With infinite forms of beauty has spread,
And no matter where we may chance to roam
Of beauty or grandeur we find the home.
Constructiveness gives the artistic skill
To chisel the marble to suit the will,
With other faculties it plays a part
In forming the wondrous pictures of art,
It gives man the power, to construct and to build,
So that the whole world with his works is filled.

Ideality gives, of beauty, the love
In the earth below, and the heavens above;
The love of beauty, wherever 'tis found,
On the mountain top or beneath the ground,
The love of beauty as one great whole
Of beauty of heart and beauty of soul;
It gives the desire to be refined,
And to possess an accomplished mind:
To imagination it gives great power
And causes it to blossom and flower,
A poet without it would lack the perfume
That charm of the soul, his wings to plume,
To enable him to soar very high
Above the earth in the star-gemmed sky.

Sublimity gives the love of the grand,
The majestic, the awful, on sea or land;
Of a mountain vast, of a yawning chasm,
Of the thunderstorm and the earthquake's spasm;
When sublimest music the soul does fill
Sublimity gives her ecstatic thrill.
Imitation mimics both nature and art,
Of the actor's talent, it forms a part,
It is large in all stars that act on the stage
And some attain fame at an early age.
In drawing and painting it greatly assists,
And copies all things that on earth exists.

In children 'tis active, causing each one
To imitate all that is said or done:
All parents this fact in their minds should bear,
And of their example take greatest care.
Mirth gives a relish for humor and fun,
It laughs and grows fat, till its day is done,
It shakes all the cobwebs out of the brain,
Thus drowning all sorrow, trouble and pain.

Human Nature closely examines each face,
The motives of men, it endeavors to trace,
In all mental powers it takes the lead
In enabling man, human minds to read.
In Shakspeare this organ was of great size,
Of his mind, 'twas the gem, the greatest prize.
Suavity makes us smooth and polite,
Both women and men it fills with delight.
Time gives the perception of duration
And waits for no man, whate'er his station,
With calculation, this power creates
A memory for both numbers and dates;
In drilling and dancing it plays its part,
And gives great aid to all musical art.
Tune gives the talent for music divine,
All melodious strains it does define,
It fills the whole world with warbling songs,
All the joys of life it greatly prolongs;

But the other powers must play their part
If one would excel in musical art.

THE PERCEPTIVE FACULTIES.

The first step, to knowledge, is observation
Of the external things of all creation,
Of their forms, sizes, colors and locations,
Their orders, numbers and variations;
The Perceptive powers to the mind brings
A knowledge of all these various things.
Above and around the eyes is their station,
Those natural inlets of observation,
It is through these windows of the brain we find
That most of our knowledge reaches the mind.

First, *Individuality* does see
A separate existence, as man, stone, tree;
Form sees the shape, and retains in the mind
An outline of each thing the eye does find.
In Cuvier this organ was of great size
And it proved to him a valuable prize.
Size, next, perceives the amount of space
An object takes up in whatever place;
It judges the weight of things by their size,
And to stock-dealers it proves a great prize:
In my travels, many of these I've found
Who could guess the weight, missing scarcely a pound.

8

Color gives the perception of tints and shades,
All artists and painters it greatly aids.
Indeed, it is not unusual to find
A man or woman that is color blind,
And many examples of these I've seen
Who not for their life could tell blue from green.
Order gives system, a place for all things,
And out of confusion arrangement brings.
Calculation gives power to calculate
In the mind, without a pencil or slate.
Locality perceives locations and places
And thus in the mind geography traces;
The surveyor and tourist it greatly does bless,
And also confers great talent for chess.

THE LITERARY FACULTIES.

The Literary organs are located
In the middle line of the forehead.
They confer on man his great gift of speech,
His power to talk, to lecture and preach,
To write, to pray, exhort and beseech,
To question, to answer, and also to teach.
First, *Language* remembers all words and names,
And these from the mouth to all it proclaims.
This organ, in orators, is of great size.
As is always shown by their prominent eyes.

Next, *Eventuality* retains events,
All actions and details it represents;
It recalls all our knowledge of the past,
And enables the mind to hold it fast;
It greatly augments the historian's power;
This organ of memory is the queen flower.

THE REFLECTIVE FACULTIES.

In the upper part of the forehead we find
These intellectual crowns of the mind.
Of all the intellectual flowers
They confer on man the grandest powers;
They investigate all nature's laws,
And endeavor of each to seek the cause.
Each action perceived by each human sense
Is traced from its cause to its consequence;
By them the greatest discoveries are made
In science and art, mechanics and trade;
Their powers range o'er a great extent,
An infinite number of things they invent.
In the whole great intellectual plan,
Greatest powers of reason are given to man.

Comparison, as its name implies,
Gives the mind great power to analyze,
To compare, classify and illustrate,
All kinds of things whether little or great;

To examine into the world's great laws,
And by analogy seek out the cause;
To put together and to take apart,
Thus greatly aiding all chemical art.
To illustrate all kinds of writings and stories
By similes, metaphors and allegories;
And when the organ is large, we find
These flowers of thought filling up the mind.
Causality plans, invents and contrives;
Down into the depths of nature it dives;
It wants a reason for all that exists,
And on a straight answer it firmly insists.
The little child looks up into your eye
And asks you to tell him the reason why;
And wants you to tell him from whence he came,
Who made him, and much more of the same.
It confers on man the power to trace
Causes to effects in whatever place
Or circumstances in which they are found,
In the heavens above or under the ground;
It gives power to reason upon all things,
And logical strength to the mind it brings.

The Perceptives see, and all facts retain,
Thus all physical qualities they explain.
The Literary retain all actions,
Words, causes, motions and transactions.

The Reflectives use, when it is desired,
All that both the other groups have acquired;
And from this data discovers the cause
Of things that exist, and defines their laws.
Now in all of this we plainly see
A beautiful mental harmony.

THE SHAPE OF THE HEAD AS INDICATIVE OF CHARACTER.

With regard to the way that the mind is read
In both young and old, from the human head,
Most people possess erroneous views,
Which now from their minds I would disabuse.
Most people believe that the human head
Has all over its surface quite thickly spread
Large numbers of little projections or lumps,
Which they call by the vulgar name of bumps.
They could just as well say blinkers for eyes,
Bread-basket for stomach, or snores for sighs.
If a man was pummeled upon his head,
He would possess bumps properly said;
And thus to any one it is plain
That bumps are not organs of the brain.
Yet most people think that by feeling the bumps,
The hills and valleys, projections and lumps,
Which they seem to think that nature has spread
All over the skull and scalp of the head,

That all traits of character can be told
In women and men, either young or old.
Now I beg leave to state this is not the case,
And all from their minds such views should erase.
We often see men who are minus their hair,
The top of whose heads are naked and bare,
As slick and as smooth as a billiard ball,
Without any bumps or projections at all;
And yet the fact is extremely plain
That they have all the organs in their brain,
And characters, too, as straight and fair
As other men who have plenty of hair.
Now from all of this we can plainly see
That there is no truth in bumpology.

The human character is always read
By the size and shape of the human head,
In connection with the temperaments,
Which bodily influence represents.
The skull has only to do with the brain
As a faithful covering of the same,
By measuring it we can always find
The size of the brain and strength of the mind.
The height, the length and the breadth of the brain
Shows the size of the organs it does contain;
The size of each organ, we always find,
Indicates the strength of each power of mind.

Thus the human mind can be always read
By actual measurements of the head.

If you find a man's head broad at the base,
Strong animal feelings you'll find in his case;
If his head be either short or long,
You will find his desires and passions strong;
And if his temperament is not slow,
He is energetic and good on the go;
If his moral organs are good as a whole,
His animal nature he will control—
And though of great force he is a good man,
A very fine type in nature's great plan.
But if he possess a low, flat head,
The moral organs are too thinly spread;
The animal rules in his mental plan,
And runs away with the whole of the man.
If you find a man's head broad above the ears,
His temper is high, and nothing he fears;
Defense and destructiveness both are large,
And with fire and spirit his mind they charge;
Prize-fighters are men who have but few fears,
And they always are broad just above the ears.
The lion and tiger, bulldog and bloodhound,
Also very wide in this region are found;
And in men of this stamp we often trace
A resemblance to them in head and face;

But if narrow the head be at the base,
A lack of spirit and force we can trace;
For steady energy we need not seek,
This part of the mind being very weak.
If the whole top head is full arched and high,
All the moral organs, which there do lie,
Are well developed, and you will find
That such a man has a virtuous mind—
You will find him honest and straight and right,
Even though in creeds he takes no delight.

If you find a man whose head up and down
Is very high from his ear to his crown,
Do not excite him, but keep quite cool,
For he is as stubborn as a mule:
He will lead very well, but will not drive;
Do not go too fast, and with him you'll thrive.
If the head is full and projecting behind,
Love of friends and family there we find;
But if the back head be narrow and flat,
There will be but very little of that;
But social sometimes we find them to be,
From self-interest or popularity.
A great deal more might be readily said
About the size and the shape of the head,
To show how beautifully it illustrates
Of human nature the various traits.

The outline is finished — so much for the plan,
This bird's-eye view of the nature of man;
Of all animal life the greatest creation,
At the head of the scale he takes his station.
Vast ages passed by before his birth,
Ere he was evolved from the dust of the earth;
Yet the finger of time, throughout that vast span,
Like an arrow did point to the coming man.
He came, and for thousands of years did roam
All over the earth, for it was his home,
And is only just now beginning to see
That there is a beautiful harmony
Between his mind and the world where he dwells,
And Phrenology the whole story tells.
Study it well, and yourself you will know,
For nature is truth, and the head will show.

THE FOUNDERS OF PHRENOLOGY.

THE first to discover the natural plan,
    And give to the world the great Science of Man,
Was a German physician of great renown,
Doctor Gaul, who was born in Tifenbrun town.
While he yet was a boy, attending the school.
Before the small world had yet called him a fool,
He happened to notice, to his great surprise,
That some of his fellows had prominent eyes:
Their eyes were so full that they seemed to project,
Or bulge out of their heads, and in this respect
They differed from others, whose eyes were depressed,
By the greater ease with which thoughts were expressed.
In fact, those with full eyes had great gift of speech,
A great flow of words, to illustrate and teach;
They remembered all words with the greatest ease,
And were such good talkers that all they could please.
From his observations the fact did arise
That all great orators had prominent eyes.
On the other hand, those whose eyes sank far back
Into their heads, in all this greatly did lack:
For their memory of words was so very bad.

That the simplest of them were all that they had
In which to express all their powers of thought—
For the reason of all this Doctor Gaul sought.
And while yet a boy all his efforts were vain,
But when a great physician he had became,
He found in the brain, to his great surprise,
The organs of language just over the eyes,

DR. GAUL.

Which, when they were large, as one might expect,
Would depress the plates, and the eyes would project.
When these organs were small they did not succeed
In depressing the plates, and the eyes did recede.
Now to Doctor Gaul's mind the fact became plain
That each power of mind had a part of the brain,
Or an organ, through which it could always act,
And to discover these he possessed great tact.

Doctor Gaul was a man of judgment and sense,
And he spared neither labor, time nor expense;
In all Europe was hardly a noted man
But of whose head Doctor Gaul had a plan;
To establish each organ these he'd compare,
And the lower animals he did not spare.

SPURZHEIM.

His whole life was spent in the study of mind,
And twenty-seven organs of brain he did find.
He laid the foundation of Phrenology,
The one natural mental philosophy;
The first in the science, and greatest in fame,
Of all by far the most illustrious name,

Upon him too much honor can never fall,
That great mental explorer, Doctor Gaul.

Next Doctor Spurzheim takes his place in the list,
And he was a great physiologist;
He was the first one to dissent from the plan
In dissecting, to slice the brain like a ham;

GEORGE COMBE.

Each fiber and part of the brain he did trace,
And thus gave to each its appropriate place.
In Brittany's Isles and in the New World
His banner of science he freely unfurled.

And next, on the list is the famous George Combe,
The greatest writer that the science has known.

He with Spurzheim, arranged a system of all
That had been discovered by Doctor Gaul.
Great powers of logic he did possess
And his thoughts were clothed in a beautiful dress,
Though his spirit has fled, his works, they still live,
And the Science of Mind, to the world they give
With all of the freshness and vigor of pen
That characterized one of earth's greatest men;
Both Spurzheim and Combe did not labor in vain
For they discovered eleven organs of the brain.

Of Americans, whom our attention claims,
Our space will admit of but very few names,
Of many bright lights, fame has had to tell; ·
Such as Boardman, Powell, and Doctor Caldwell,
All men, whose bright talents have left their mark,
Whose memory can never fade or grow dark,
And last, but not least, in the annals of fame,
Is another great light, familiar his name;
With energy, force, and talent combined.
He devoted his life to blessing mankind;
The great truths of Science he spread o'er the world,
And to thousands this banner of light was unfurled.
But a short time ago he worked with a will,
And now, both his tongue and his pen are still,
For the Angel of Death took him by the hand
And led him away to that Beautiful Land.

S. R. WELLS.

Although *Wells* has gone, his Journal still lives,
And still to the world the great truths it gives,
It spreads the good tidings from hand to hand,
And thus blesses thousands all over the land.
As the world progresses in science and art
The works of these heroes will play a great part;
And although to fame they are well known now,
Yet, still, greater laurels will heap on each brow;
That this is the case we invariably find
With all those who labor to bless mankind.

CHARLIE AND I.

CHARLIE and I, we both worked on the farm,
  Each day of our life, had for us a charm,
And there was nothing our hearts to alarm,
For we were healthy and strong.
Charlie and I, we both plowed in the corn
With go-devil plows, that now look forlorn;
For honest labor we never did scorn,
And thus we worked all day long.

Charlie and I, as we labored did sing,
Though we kept no tune it was just the thing;
And oft to the winds all care we did fling,
For we were happy and gay.
Charlie and I, we both plowed in the corn,
Beginning our work in the early morn,
As happy grangers as ever were born;
Happy at work, or at play.

Charlie and I were a-plowing one day
Near the side of the road, that passed that way,
When we stopped to rest, to talk, and to play,
For we felt jolly that day;

While Charlie and I were there sitting down,
A long line of buggies, came from the town,
And passed us by, as the road they went down,
A picnic party so gay.

The buggies were filled with ladies, so fair,
All decked with bright plumage and ribbon gemmed hair,
And stylish young men with them to compare,
Forming a gorgeous array.
To Charlie and I this was a surprise,
We got up and stared with all of our eyes;
As they faded from sight the corn heard two sighs,
A bright cloud darkened our day.

While Charlie and I were thus standing there,
Some runners drove by, with a careless air,
Puffing cigar smoke up into the air;
They seemed so rakish and gay.
Both Charlie and I, we again sat down,
Lawyers and doctors rode by from the town,
Smoking cigars, as on us they looked down;
Says Charlie, "This does not pay."

Says Charlie to me, "This never will do,
To be a clod-hopper all my life through,

I'll try something else, so better had you;
We can do better, I say."
Says Charlie, "I will a profession learn,
I'll sit in my office and money earn,
And in my carriage cigars I will burn;
I tell you that is the way."

Says Charlie to me, "It will be great fun
To take life so easy from sun to sun,
To have all great people after me run;
I'll be a big man, you see."
Says I to Charlie, "You are talking sense,
Set up the cigars, who cares for expense?"
And I ran and jumped right over the fence,
I felt so happy and free.

Says I to Charlie, "I'll travel about,
At the great hotels you'll find me hang out
And thousands of people will hear me spout;
Oh! that will be fun for me."
Says I to Charlie, "I'll lead a gay life,
I'll go to the picnic and get me a wife,
I will bid farewell to this dirty strife;
A brilliant couple you'll see."

Says I to Charlie, "I'll cover her o'er
With beautiful gems, from a foreign shore,
And then through the world away we will soar;
Oh, will not that splendid be!"
Says Charlie to me, "Do not be so fast,
We will work this year, it will not long last,
And then our farming will be of the past,
We will be forever free."

With Charlie and I the years, they have fled,
Since we left the farm they have quickly sped,
Each followed the aim, by which he was led,
We both climbed up a small hill.
Brother Charlie now sits and money earns,
He rides in his carriage, cigars he burns,
Of his trade he knows all the quirks and turns,
Of all this he has his fill.

But Charlie finds out his work is not play,
He cudgels his brain, by night and by day,
He can get no rest, the devil's to pay,
For people will always come.
And as for myself, I travel about,
At the big hotels I often hang out,
And thousands of people do hear me spout,
It is not such awful fun.

Both Charlie and I look back to the farm,
To those happy days, which had such a charm,
To our spring-time of life so bright and warm,
And feel both pleasure and pain.
Both Charlie and I, as Billings does claim,
From the top of our little hills of fame
Look down in the valley from whence we came,
And wish we were back again.

THE PRISONER OF DARKNESS.

IF in any of your rambles
  Through the country, town, or city,
You should see a lonely mansion
That with age is growing yellow,
Round which sunbeams glide with sorrow,
Round which moonbeams glide with pity.

With its windows, sealed and boarded,
With no crack or crevice shallow
To admit the brilliant sunlight,
To admit the gentle moonlight,
To admit the gentle zephyr,
To admit the breath of nature;
All without, is desolation,
All within, a dreary darkness,
Darkness reigns there, reigns forever

Should a passer-by inform you
That a living, human being
In those halls, of utter darkness,
Was engulfed, entombed forever;
Dark before him, dark behind him,
Darkness on all sides prevailing,

Dark above him, dark below him,
Darkness curtained all around him;
Like a caged bird he had fluttered,
Tried to break the chains that bound him;
But the darkness was unchanging,
And its blackness was unfading.

Shines the brilliant sun at morning.
Beams the gentle moon at evening,
Nightfall gilds the heavens with glory,
Gems the sky with starry flowers;
But the prisoner, walled in darkness,
Cannot feel the holy blessing;
Sun and moon, and stars are shining,
Pouring forth their golden showers,
But no gilded ray can reach him,
And no light can he discover.

And all nature, it is lovely,
Beauties scattered in profusion,
Birds and blossoms, leaves and flowers,
Mountains grand, primeval forests
In harmonious confusion,
But he never can behold them.
Father, mother, sister, brother,
He will never see your faces
Till the angel blows his trumpet,

Till the dead are resurrected,
Till the world is called to judgment;
Then the light will shine before him,
Then the light will shine behind him,
Then the light will shine above him.
Then the light will shine below him;
Spread its glories all around him,
And its rays, they are unchanging,
And its brightness is unfading.

THE MISSOURIAN AND HIS MOTHER-IN-LAW.

YES; I've bin married twict, Professor, I'm a livin'
    with number two,
The fust, she war a heap more slender, and I reckon
    purtier too;
Her eyes war as grey as a rabbit, and her har was a purty
    brown,
Her fetures war smoothlike, an reg'lar, an' she had much
    larnin' tuck down,
Of the two, she was the most graceful, fer she had such a
    purty way,
An' when I used fer to go courtin', she'd coom to the door
    and she'd say,
"Why, Jim, I'm so glad fer to see you, take a cher by the
    stove, that's right,
Fer of late I'm feelin' quite lonely, I'm right glad you've
    come here to-night.
You are lookin' so well an' hearty; have you jist come up
    from the farm?
How are all of the folks down your way? Let 'em talk,
    they'll do us no harm."

An' all of the time she was smilin', an' lookin' so purty
    an' sweet,
That it set my heart all to bilin' an' it seemed like I'de
    fall at her feet.
Fer more nor a year her I courted, an' was happy as man
    could be,
An' I would hev courted her longer, but then we war
    married, you see:
Fer her mammy didn't like long engagements, the shorter
    the better, said she;
She tuck that hull thing on her shoulders, an that was
    what jist sooted me.
She sed there was no use of foolin' an' sittin' up late every
    nite,
Mite as well be married in airnest, an' myself agreed with
    her quite.
I'd a never hed spunk to ask her for to splice with a man
    like me,
Fer she seemed a Angel above me, en' me clair below her,
    you see;
There was sich a distance atween us, that fer me she
    seemed much too good;
I couldn't git up to war she was, an' that was jist whar
    I stood,
Fer she was so smart an' so high-flown, an' I hed no larnin'.
    you see,

An' I felt kinder 'shamed to ask her to splice with a feller
    like me;

Fer you see I was kinder awkward, hedn't bin to the
    dancin' skule,

An' when we both went out to parties, I reckon, I looked
    like a fool.

But thin the old woman, her mammy (for that time she
    sided with me),

Seemed to see the fix that I wos in, an' did the hull
    bizness, you see.

I tell you we hed a big weddin', an' the neighbors they all
    cum in,

An' if ever a man was happy, the name of that man, it
    was Jim.

Fer my boots, they would hardly hold me, an' I seemed
    chuck full of new life

As I rode away in the buggy, to my farm with my purty
    wife.

No she ain't dead at all, Perfessor, or leastways, she warn't,
    I know,

Fer I red a letter she'd written, lem me see, jist a year ago.

Oh! no; she don't live in these parts, she's done gone fer
    more nor five years,

You see a heap of trouble I've hed, I kin hardly keep back
    the tears

When I think of all that I've bin through, of all that I've
    gained an I've lost.

'Fore a man picks out a mother-'n-law he'd best figger up
    all the cost.

As I tole you before, Perfessor, when I fust married Mary
    Jane

An' I tuck her down to the farm-house; yes, sir, that was
    my fust wife's name,

An' fer five long years we war happy, as happy as happy
    could be;

An' I thought it would be so allers, but that warn't the
    case, you see.

We had two of as purty children, as you cud find in any
    town,

A boy an' a girl, how we loved 'em an' we toted 'em up
    and down.

But Mary Jane's father, he sickened an' soon was put under
    the ground,

Then mother-'n-law came down to our place an' sed, she
    was gwine to board 'round

Among her different sons-in-law, an' as I was nearest, you
    see,

She reckon she'd cum down to our place for to try it a
    spell with me.

Of course, I felt very much tickled as also did my Mary
    Jane,

Fer to hev her cum fust to our place was a heap of honor
    to claim;

An' we did all we could to please her, fer we both thought
    it mighty fine

To hev a gran'mammy to our place, an' to hev her fer a
    long time.

Fer a time things went on as us'al, jist the same as they
    allus had,

But after a spell I did notice, that Mary Jane seemed to
    feel bad.

Onct I put my arm right around her, an' ask'd her if I
    hed done wrong,

But she shuck me off mighty spiteful, an' sed "Lem me
    be," go along,

I tell you what, that was a stunner, an' it nearly fetched
    out the tears,

'Twas the fust time she'd hurt my feelin's in all of those
    five happy years,

Although I hed little book larnin', one thing I could see
    square and plain,

That she never used me so cool-like, 'til after the old
    woman came.

Fer when I used for to go plowin' she'd call me back
    more'n half a mile

Fer to git off a good joke on me, an' to play fer quite a
    long while,

An' although she kept me from workin' I felt good an'
    didn't care fer that;
But after the old woman cum there, I was never called
    back, that's flat.
She war'nt the same that she hed bin, an' begun fer to
    treat me cool,
An' when I tried fer to git near her she would shy off jist
    like a mule;
At last I got tired of trying, but kept on to work jist the
    same,
An' I couldn't see what in blazes hed got into my Mary
    Jane.
But one day she spoke right up to me; says she, "Jim,
    this will never do,
Fer you look so ragged and slouching; I's a fool for marryin'
    you;
Now, why don't you try an' spruce up like, an' git you a
    new suit of clo'es?
Be in style like Sprigins an' Flasher, you're rich enough,
    that we both 'no's,
And as for myself, I've no dresses, no duds, that are fit to
    be seen
Except that last silk that you got me, an' that is an old,
    nasty green.
Yes, I thought it nice when you got it, but that was a
    long time ago,

Afore my dear mother came down here, but now things
    are altered, you know.
An' mother, too, needs some new dresses, if you had the
    soul of a mouse
You'd do all these things you had orto, an' fix up this
    horrid old house.
I'm so glad that mother's cum down here, fer five years
    I didn't know my rights,
But I reckon I'm gettin' wiser, for mother has told me
    sich sights."

If a cannon burst or an earthquake, to me, 'twould hev bin
    jist the same,
I wouldn't hev thought it was in her, for I thought she
    was kinder tame.
Says I, "Mary Jane, I'm conceited, but I think I look jist
    as nice
As any of them other fellows, that you had a chance fer to
    splice;
I've got a good suit of grey woolins as in any town can
    be found,
An' you an' your mammy dress better than any of the
    neighbors 'round;
An' as for that Sprigins an' Flasher, they're dandies that
    live in the town,
An' if I shu'd try to dress like 'em 'twould make me look
    jist like a clown:

An' as fer this house that we live in, you thought it a
    very nice one,
You said 'twas too good to live in afore your dear mammy
    did come.
An' she aint doin' right I tell you, a putting sich things
    in your head,
She had better mind her own bizness an' keep a tight
    tongue in her head."
Then Mary Jane burst out a-cryin' an' tumbled right onto
    the floor,
An soon she was kickin' an screechin, she never hed done
    so before.
It made me feel orful to see her, an' her mammy came
    rushin' in,
I tell you, Perfessor, it was orful the way they pitched
    into poor Jim.
I didn't hold out long aginst 'em afore to their wish I cum
    down,
I told 'em, I'd hitch up the buggy an' snake 'em both up
    to the town,
An' then they could buy all the dresses, I'd give 'em both
    leave to wade in,
An' when they had finished the bizness, jist tell 'em to
    charge it to Jim;
An' I'd git me a suit of broadcloth, a big stovepipe hat, an'
    a cane,

I'd do anything to be happy agin with my own Mary Jane.
But I was a fool for doin' it, fer if I had stood my own
ground,
They wouldn't hev thought me a puppy, an' nosed me
'round an' around.
Some men they are mean in their families, an' some would
be mean if they could,
But it often does spile a woman for a husband to be too
good;
Fer leastways it did in my own case, it spilt Mary Jane
fer a wife,
An' I was henpecked in the household; oh, didn't I lead
a sweet life!
Thar was a big change down to our place, two dressmakers
cum up from town,
Thar was heaps of dry goods an' sich like, all over the
house layin' 'roun',
An' carpenters, too, war kept busy, a fixin' most every day,
An' the pile of money I'd saved up began fer to dwindle
away,
I thought that they never'd git through it, fer to give me
a resting spell,
Fer they nosed me 'round like a poodle, an' my house it
seemed like a hell.
But you see there's an end of all things, an' soon they
both wanted a change;

10

So Mary Jane cum to me one day, says she, Jim, we want
    to arrange
Fer a house you're to buy in the town, an' jist furnish it
    up to a T,
An' give it to my dearest mother, she wants to live up
    thar' you see;
Fer what is the use of nice dresses an' the other nice
    things, you know,
When we are cl'ar out in the country, whar thar's no one
    to see the show,
But if mother has a house down town, I ken go an' visit,
    you see,
An' thar I ken show off my fine clo'es, and so happy we
    all will be.
I jumped at that chance I ken tell you, an' that very day
    I went down
An' I bought an' rigged up a nice house right square in
    the middle of town.
It tuck all the rest of my greenbacks, but fer that I keard
    not a straw,
I knew I'd the best of the bargain to git rid of my moth-
    er-'n-law.
Next day bag an' baggage I moved her, and thought I was
    happy fer life;
An', then we war alone at our place, an' Mary Jane
    seemed like my wife,

An' we both begun to be happy, and things they grew
    brighter each day.
Fer though she went oft to her mammy's, she didn't fer
    a long time stay.
But in three months somethin' did happen an' it made me
    feel mighty rough,
Fer mother-'n-law came down to our place, and sed she'd
    been lonesome enough.
She had brought her bed an' her baggage, and to me the
    fact it was plain
That she was agin on my shoulders, and thar she was
    bound to remain;
But like a rat-dog up I sprunted, I bundled her back to
    the town,
I tell you it was orful, the screechin', but fer onct I put
    my foot down.
Mary Jane with the children followed, an' fer six months
    I was alone,
But in some respects I felt better than I had since moth-
    er-'n-law cum.
I missed Mary Jane an' the children, but I kept to work
    jist the same,
Till that long six months was over, and then she cum
    back agin;
An' sed she was sorry she'd left me, and she'd make me
    a better wife,

An' then onct agin I was happy an' looked on the bright
    side of life.

But soon she did git quite uneasy an' urged me to mort-
    gage the farm,

Fer to try my luck at store-keeping, fer she sed it could
    do no harm.

An' this time she coaxed me so purty, fer my life I couldn't
    say no.

So I mortgaged the farm, bought a store, and into the
    town we did go;

Well, the bizness, it clim' rite onto me, an' all of the peo-
    ple cum in,

Fer I always did hev a good name, an' they all said they'd
    trade with Jim.

An' I soon would hev made my fortin' if they would hev
    jist lem me be,

But Mary Jane was thick with her mammy, and that was
    the trouble you see.

I could see that she felt above me, fer she used me jist like
    a dog,

An' now'days she trampled upon me jist as if I was an
    old log,

When I'd bin in the bizness a year, I sha'n't never forgit
    that day,

Mary Jane hed fer me a surprise; says she, "Jim, I've
    somethin' to say,

Thar is no use of livin' like this, we can't git along anyhow,

Jim, I thought that I did love you onct, but you see I
    don't love you now,

You hev done jist the best that you could, but you never
    was proud you see.

An' now both mother an' I, we think that you shouldn't
    have spliced with me:

Fer you never could be my equal if you should try ever
    so much,

Fer you hain't got quality in you, an' your great-grand-
    father was Dutch.

Jim, we've lived long enough together, it is time fer to
    part, of course,

An' I want you to see the lawyers an' hev 'em make out
    a divorce,

You must give me four thousand dollars, with your biz-
    ness, 'tain't much to pay:

You ken hev your pick of the children, they're about equal
    any way.

We are goin' to Californy, that is, both my mother an' me;

An' won't bother you any longer, fer the last of us you
    will see."

I hed got quite used to the changes, but this was the big-
    gest of all,

I knew it would wind up the bizness, fer it was the wo'st
    that could fall.

Says I, "Mary Jane, I've been faithful an' dun all my duty
 by you;
I hev loved and never ken hate you, but the divorce I will
 put through,
You sha'n't live with a man that shames you, fer only a
 very short while.
Mary Jane, you are good in figgers fer you hev jist sized
 all my pile,
If I give you four thousand dollars I'll hev nothin' left
 but the farm.
With an orful big mortgage on it, which I guess will keep
 it from harm.
I will take my little girl Sally, fer the boy, he is more like you,
He might get 'shamed of his father an' want a divorce put
 through.
You ken go off to Californy or you ken go over the sea,
But you can't cum back to whar I am, fer Jim, he's goin'
 to be free.
In the future when you git older, you'll, may be, look back
 and you'll see
Jist how lucky you was in choosing atween your dear
 mammy an' me."

Yes, they both went to Californy, leaving me right in this
 'ere town,
An' the farm was all that I had left with a mortgage to
 hold it down:

But I went back an' lived upon it, an' I started all over agin,
If ever a fellow was lonesome, I tell you that fellow was
  Jim.
Then I got acquainted with Jennie, fer she was an or-
  phling you see,
An' thar couldn't be a mother-n-law in splicing with one
  like she,
An' in jist one year we were married, from the leavin' of
  Mary Jane,
An' Jennie, she dotes her eyes on me, which is a good
  deal fer to claim.
She ain't quite so purty as 'tother, but she is nobler an'
  better, too.
An' she never has got to changin' or tryin' to poodle me
  through,
Fer Jennie ain't one of the high-flown, nor one of the
  stuck-up kind,
But she makes me a good, faithful wife, an' she's always
  the same, I find,
But when I do think of Mary Jane, it gives me sich a
  funny thrill,
The fust one we love always seems to hev a power over
  us still.
If any man wants to enjoy life an' keep out of the devil's
  claws,
He must look out an' steer his raft cl'ar of all of the
  mother-'n-laws.

BOB, WILL, AND I.

WE were three chums. Bob, Will, and I,
  For we were boys together,
And memory often breathes a sigh
  For all our past spring weather.
We were three links in friendship's chain,
  And side by side we wandered;
Oh, shall we ever meet again
  Ere all our days are squandered?

'Tis many years since we did part
  In Dave'port's gay city —
Each went his way with heavy heart,
  And two were full of pity.
For one of us misfortune's breath
  Had seared and scorched and blighted
In such a way that until death
  The harm could not be righted.

Here is my hand, old Bob and Will,
  Though parted far asunder,

We still can feel true friendship's thrill—
　All distance stands from under.
I grasp your hands, my friends so dear,
　We shake with hearty feeling,
I seem to hear your words of cheer
　Upon my fancy stealing.

A RIDE TO THE CHICAGO BOULEVARDS.

FROM the center of the city
    To the boulevard we glide,
And the moonlight and the starlight
    Stream upon us as we ride.
Through the avenues so stately,
    Flanked by many a costly pile,
Palaces of wealth and comfort
    Flitting by us file on file.

Through the plate glass of the windows
    We catch glimpses as we pass
Of the dramas that are acting
    Just behind the crystal glass.
There are women, men and children
    Lounging in the easy chairs,
For it is the Sabbath evening,
    And there is a rest from cares.

There are pictures, there are statues
    Gazing on each group below;
Gems of art and flowers of beauty;
    While each room is all aglow

With the brilliance of the gas-light
   Sparkling o'er each varied scene,
Forming two great panoramas,
   As we glide along between.

But the South Park we are nearing,
   Now we strike the level track,
And the horses, bounding forward,
   Send the still air rushing back.
Faster, faster we are whizzing,
   Like a rocket through the night,
On our left the trees are whirling,
   Pictured flowers on our right.

Now we turn — this is the forest —
   Silence broods, there's not a sound,
And we feel the breath of nature
   As the shadows gather round.
What a change from all the bustle
   Of the city's roar and jam;
Here's no ringing, hooting, howling,
   But instead a peaceful calm.

Now we turn our faces homeward,
   O'er the grand boulevards we scud.
For the horses well remember
   'Tis the place to show their blood.

Soon we reach the beauteous lakeside,
　　A grand scene bursts on our eye,
A vast mirror in the moonlight,
　　Looking like an under sky.

From its bosom stars are shining
　　Back to moon and stars above;
In the distance both are blending
　　Like two hearts when filled with love.
Now we plunge into the city,
　　And we mingle with its roar,
For our glorious ride is over,
　　And dull care returns once more.

EXTRACTS FROM THE PRESS.

Rocheport, Missouri, *Enterprise:* Prof. Bronson is one of the best phrenologists now traveling, his lectures are intensely interesting and instructive, he delineates character with lifelike accuracy.

Sioux City, Iowa, *Daily Journal:* Prof. C. H. Bronson, the Blind Phrenologist, delivered his first of a course of lectures of four last evening, in the Methodist Episcopal church. Seasoning his lecture richly with mirth, it made it both instructive and amusing.

Unionville, Missouri, *Ledger:* Prof. Bronson, the celebrated Blind Phrenologist, delivered a free lecture last night, introductory to a course of lectures which he is delivering at the Christian Church in this place. The Professor is a rare speaker and should be heard by every one.

Trenton, Missouri, *Grundy County Times:* Prof. Bronson, the Blind Phrenologist, has been delivering a series of lectures here this week. He draws full houses, and is kept busy during the daytime giving private examinations at his room. He is a clear, forcible and witty speaker, and has a thorough knowledge of his subject. At his public examinations given at the close of his lectures, he unfolds the character of his subjects with a correctness which astonishes the audience. If you have weak points don't go near the Professor, or else go as Nicodemus went to Christ, secretly.

Benham, Texas, *North Texas Enterprise:* Prof. Bronson delivered several very interesting lectures on the science of Phrenology last week, and had a good hearing every night, notwithstanding the weather was very unfavorable the last two nights. The Professor certainly understands the science, and we liked his views upon the subject better than any we ever heard expressed by any lecturer upon the same. His lectures all had a moral and religious tendency, and no one could object to anything advanced by him. His eulogy upon woman was certainly eloquent in the extreme, and we thought that he spoke the sentiments of his heart, for the lady that has cast her fortunes with him is certainly a helpmeet in the true sense of the term. We wish them a cordial reception wherever their lots may be cast.

Oswego, Kansas, *Independent:* Prof. Bronson, the Blind Phrenologist, has been delivering a series of very instructive and humorous lectures at the Baptist church the past week. His rendition of character is remarkable for accuracy, not because of his being blind, but because of its truthfulness, and to our

certain knowledge is far more accurate in his delineations than the leading phrenologists of the country. We are free to admit that since we have attended his
lecture and have heard him portray the character and measure the talent of dozens
of persons with whom we are personally acquainted, that we are far less skeptical in
recognizing phrenology as a science than we were before the advent of the Blind
Phrenologist. At the close of each lecture he shampooed from two to a dozen
ladies and gentlemen. Mr. Frank Parsons won the prize as the best lady's man,
and Miss Belle Wells as the handsomest young lady in the audience. At last
accounts no Websterian fossils were discovered.

Paris, Texas, *Common Sense:* **Prof. Bronson,** a blind phrenologist, lectured the
other night at the Christian church. There was a big crowd of ladies and gentlemen present. At the close of the lecture a committee was appointed to select
candidates for examination. The lucky man was Dr. Felix Johnson, Cumberland
Presbyterian pastor, of this city. The blind man of science proceeded to say that
the doctor was very fond of the fair sex; in fact, as Josephus says of Solomon,
"immoderately fond of the women;" that if his wife was to die he would lose no
time in looking out for another; that he had a splendid appetite, loved good
eating, and liked to "dine out," and was sure to make it understood, when he
did, that Dr. Johnson was there, etc. Some one in the audience wanted to know
about his religion. The sightless scientist resumed: "Publicly he is very religious,
but privately he is not troubled with piety; he has a fine mechanical head, and
while he would make but a sorry preacher, he would make a fine blacksmith."
Here the doctor turned very red in the face, and said: "Sir, I have been a preacher
of the Gospel for forty years!" The blind man shook his head, as much as to say,
"That is too thin" During the whole time the audience were in a roar, and the
fun was prodigious!

Iowa City, Iowa, *Daily Press:* We had a call yesterday from Prof. Henry
B. onson, the Blind Phrenologist. He was reared in Iowa City, and so, aside
from old friendship and fellowship, we feel honest pride in his success. Years
ago, while a student of the University, he became totally blind. He was a lad
of slender physique, and it would seem that with sight gone his career was
ended and nothing promised but despair. The slender boy has, however, made
his life such a success that its story deserves place in the annals of the world.
Using readers, he began the study of themes upon which Gall, Spurzheim and
Combe first enlightened the world; even peering without eyes into the philosophy of Lavater, until now he is the most successful of American lecturers upon
psychological subjects and science of the mind. His tours cover East, West
and South, and success follows merit wherever he appears. Happily mated
with a wife who enters into plans to help them on, the blind student finds himself before he is thirty years old strongly entrenched in the esteem of scholars,
sought by the public, in possession of a comfortable income. Contrast this
with the weakness of that sudden darkness years ago which seemed to have
reduced life to a groping bondage to the bare needs that would sustain it.

PUBLICATIONS OF S. R. WELLS & CO.

I would respectfully call the attention of the public to

THE PHRENOLOGICAL JOURNAL AND SCIENCE OF HEALTH. Price reduced from $3 to $2 a year.

These two Journals, having been combined, are now published **as one**, and the Science of Human Character, the Laws which govern the Physical Organism, and the Relations of Mental and Physical Health to External Conditions, are the grand themes which belong to the special province of this Magazine, and are treated of in it from points of view embraced by no other serial publication.

PHRENOLOGY unfolds the relations of Mind and its physical instrumentalities; shows how the multifold diversities of human character and capacity are related to universal laws, and by a positive analysis of individual mentality ministers to individual usefulness, designating special aptitude, and indicating the methods by which mental and physical deficiencies may be remedied. As an agency in training the young, in correcting and reforming the vicious, and in controlling the insane, its value cannot be estimated.

It treats also of ETHNOLOGY, or the Natural History of Man; contains practical articles on PHYSIOLOGY, DIET, EXERCISE, and the LAWS OF LIFE AND HEALTH; Portraits, Sketches, and Biographies of the Leading Men and Women of the World, besides much general and useful information on the leading topics of the day. It is intended to be the most interesting and instructive *Family Magazine* published.

TERMS.— Published monthly at $2 a year, single numbers 20 cents.

Since my early boyhood I have been a constant reader of the Journal, and it has been of inestimable value to me. It is pure and elevating in its character. No family should be without it. Now is the time to subscribe. Hand in your names to Mrs. B. or my agent, or send above price to S. R. WELLS & Co., No. 737 Broadway, New York.

In order to answer the numerous inquiries as to what works give the best general idea of Phrenology and Physiognomy, I call special attention to the following list:

COMBE (GEORGE)—

A SYSTEM OF PHRENOLOGY, with one hundred engravings. $1.50.

THE CONSTITUTION OF MAN—Considered in Relation to External Objects. With Portrait. $1.50.

LECTURES ON PHRENOLOGY. With an Essay on the Phrenological Mode of Investigation, and a Historical Sketch. By ANDREW BOARDMAN, M.D. $1.50.

MORAL PHILOSOPHY; The Duties of Man in his Individual, Domestic and Social Capacities. $1.50.
    Uniform edition. 4 vols. **Extra cloth. $5.00.**
    Library edition. 4 vols. **$10.00.**

WARD'S
NATURAL SCIENCE ESTABLISHMENT,

ROCHESTER, NEW YORK.

I desire to call special attention of all students of Zoology and Geology, lecturers, teachers, etc., to HENRY A. WARD's vast collection specimens, which fully illustrate every department of Natural History, embracing fossils of all animals and plants from every quarter of the globe. Also skeletons of mammals, birds, reptiles and fishes, both stuffed and mounted; invertebrates of all kinds, corals, shells, starfish, sea-eggs, etc.; in fact, models and specimens of all the varied forms of life from the photozoan up to man. Altogether, it embraces the largest collection in the United States. These specimens are kept constantly on hand, and are for sale at reasonable prices. I have a collection of them which I obtained from Mr. WARD, and which can be seen at the lecture-room.

Everything that comes from his establishment is skillfully prepared, and just what it is represented to be.

For catalogues of prices, etc., address HENRY A. WARD, Rochester, New York.

C. H. BRONSON.

ATTENTION.—*The foregoing notices were placed in this work voluntarily by the author. unsolicited by either firm.*